Dual Souls

SHADOW

Nicholas Sumonja

PAGE PUBLISHING, INC.
Conneaut Lake, PA

First originally published by Page Publishing 2019

ISBN 978-1-64701-148-2 (pbk)
ISBN 978-1-64701-149-9 (digital)

Printed in the United States of America

Dedicated to my friends and family who got me through my own dark times and made this possible. Also to my real-life Alex, you know who you are.

Chapter One

"Come on, Sam, the party's started already!" Alex, my best friend, shouted at me through my bedroom door.

"Why don't you go on without me?" I suggested. I sat on my bed as my anxiety set in. "You'll have more fun if I'm not there to drag you down."

"I'm not going to this one without you." I heard a thud on the wall as he leaned back against it. "I told you I was going to take you to a party in our senior year, and this may be the best one"—he paused—"it's at a lake. I know you love water."

"Alex, just leave the freak if he wants to be a recluse!" Megan, his girlfriend, bellowed from downstairs.

"I'm not leaving my best friend behind this time!" he shouted back. I heard footsteps storming up the stairs, followed by a pounding on the door.

"Sam, get over yourself and get out here!" I jumped as Megan screamed through the door. "Think of us for once. I'm the head cheerleader, and your best friend is the varsity quarterback. This is the biggest party of our senior year. If we don't show up, it'll be disastrous."

"Breathe, Megan," I heard Alex chimed in and stepped between us, as usual.

"If you're that concerned, take my car keys and go." I heard the keys jingle and a sigh from Megan. "Look, I'll get him to come with me. We'll take his car there. You screaming at him isn't going to help matters."

"Whatever," she said before the keys jingled again. "You better make it before it gets dark." I heard her footsteps as she went down the stairs and the front door opened and slammed shut.

"All right, dude, it's just you and me," Alex continued and knocked on the door. "Can I come in?"

"It's not locked, Alex," I answered and saw him smiling as he opened the door.

"She's right, you know."

"Who? Megan?" He sat down on the bed next to me. "You know, she's just impatient and doesn't understand."

I leaned against the headboard. "But, she's right. I'm a freak."

"So what if you are?"—he raised his voice—"So what if you overanalyze everything? You stress so much to make yourself sick sometimes. We *all* have our quirks dude. You've just gotta learn to deal with it. Keep those who love you close, in spite of that. And forget all those who throw you to the curb because of it." He stood up and held out his hand. "Now, get up and let's go have a good time." He smiled. I hesitated for a moment before taking his hand. He glanced down at the crescent shaped birthmark on my hand.

"You might consider getting that checked someday." He laughed, pulling me out of my room and out the front door.

"Why? If it was cancerous, I would be gone already."

The look he shot me as I got in the car showed that I went too far.

"Sorry," I quickly blurted out.

"Not cool, man," he snapped. "You know how I feel about losing people since my family died in that fire."

"I know. I'm sorry, I-I just…," I stammered, remembering the fire that took both our families six months back.

"No, I get it." His face softened. "I was in that dark place and lost for a long time." We pulled into a spot at the lake from where I noticed all the people. "Then, someone pointed out some bright spots to shed some light into the darkness." He nudged me. "We still have each other. We were both over eighteen, so neither of us had to go into foster care. The insurance claims were enough for us to keep my family's house, so we weren't homeless. It's like everything fell neatly in place. Softened the blow as much as possible."

"Alex!" Someone from the team spotted us and waved. "You made it!"

Alex waved back politely as the kid went back to his conversation. Megan walked by and waved as she and the rest of the cheer squad headed toward the lake.

"We need to get you to realize that the whole world isn't out to get you," Alex continued, "there *are* good people out there. Get out of your shell, man." He patted my back. "Now, come on and let's go have some fun. I'll stay close to you the whole time." He stepped out and walked around. Alex stood by the door and waited for me to come out. I sighed one final time before opening the door and followed him into the crowd. We barely made it to the food table before the football team came to greet him.

"Dude, what took you so long?" one of the players asked. I recognized him: Dustin Arrow, star running back of our team.

"Even Megan beat you here, and she's always *fashionably late*." A player I didn't recognized said, slapping Alex's back, and they broke out into a laugh.

"What, a guy can't oversleep?" he said, covering for me, and the whole team laughed again.

"Guys, you've met my roommate Sam, right?" They all murmured a confused affirmation. "Guess not then." He threw his arm around me and said, "Guys, this is Samuel Nogard. Sam, these are the guys." We all exchanged nods and murmured hellos.

"Alex, let's go throw the ball around," Dustin said, flinging the football at Alex, who caught it with ease.

"I don't know, guys." Alex said tossing the ball back at him, looking at me for a brief second.

"Go ahead, man. I'll go chill by the lake or something," I said and smiled the best smile I could manage. I couldn't ruin the fun for him.

"You sure, man? I mean, I promised you," he muttered, feeling guilty.

"And I'm sure you'll keep it after you finish throwing the ball around." I said keeping the smile plastered on my face.

"You can join us if you want," one of the players offered. I saw Dustin roll his eyes slightly. "I mean, it's just for fun, right?" He glared down Dustin for his behavior.

"It's cool," I replied, pointing toward the lake with a drink in my hand. "I'm gonna go chill by the water." I felt Alex staring at me as I walked toward the lake at an even pace. So I threw my hand up to wave and shouted back, "Have fun, guys!" I walked along the shore till I found a secluded spot where I could people-watch. I kicked off my sandals and dipped my feet into the water, stopping only for a moment to adapt to the cold. I took a sip from my drink and began to look around. I watched Alex tossing a pass to Dustin, and Dustin catching it without stopping. I saw some kids playing volleyball in the sand pit. I laughed out loud when I spotted Megan being pushed into the water by another cheerleader. She, in turn, got pulled in by Megan. I turned back to the lake and watched the waves glisten in the warm spring day. I smiled as I reminisced the first time I came here.

I had begged my mom and dad all week to take me swimming, and finally they caved in. Mom said that Dad would take Alex and me to the lake on the weekend if his parents OK'd it. I was so excited when my mom picked up the phone and called Mrs. Sutherman. She told her it'd be a boy's weekend, and she would stay back to watch Emily, my baby sister. Mom reminded her that Dad was a trained EMT, and we would be in very good hands, swimming at our young age. That argument and Alex's loud pleading on the other end got her to finally yield. The three of us had a blast that weekend. Dad fixed hamburgers on the grill which Mom had prepared. I watched in amazement as the raw meat patties turned brown.

Alex and I had nearly given my dad a heart attack when we discovered the air pocket under one of the docks. I couldn't help but laugh when he hit his head on the bottom of the dock, breaking the surface of the water when he came to search for us. That was the only time my dad had spanked me, and he made us promise not to tell anyone he had lost us.

"Nothing can ever come close to the burgers your parents had made for us the first time we came out here." A sudden voice snapped me out of my daydream. I turned to see Alex walking down toward me.

I lay on my back and stared up at the clouds. "Busted, huh? And how'd you know what I was thinking about?"

"Because I know you," he answered, lying down beside me. "I brought you here to get you out of your shell, dude. You need to go socialize."

"I've done enough talking to the masses today, thank you." I turned and stared at him. "Besides, you told me you were bringing me here to have fun, and believe it or not, I am."

"I know you are, dude," he laughed. "I'm just trying to help. I mean, who knows what's going to happen after graduation." He sat up and stared at the water. "I mean, the guys want me to attend State with them on scholarship, which sounds nice. Our inheritance nest egg won't diminish on tuition." I sat up, feeling the sudden emotion switch. "Megan wants me to go to the community college downtown with her. That's too far of a commute, and you—"

"Will be fine," I finished reassuring him as much as I could.

"You haven't applied anywhere though, man, even if it's for a job"—he paused—"this is a big year for us, and…I just worry about you. That's all."

"And I thank you for it." I skipped a stone into the lake. "Look, you know I aced my ACTs and SATs. I can write and b.s. as well as the next person. If I decide to go somewhere, I will." I started to put my shoes back on. "Look, I don't know what our future holds, but I do know this: No matter what happens, we will get through it together even if we are in different states. You got my back, and I've got yours, always."

He smiled at me and was about to say something when we heard a sudden scream from the far end of the lake. We exchanged a nod before taking off toward the scream.

"That sounded like one of the cheerleaders!" he shouted as we ran. As we got closer, I saw two creatures laughing and our classmates freaked out. One was a fly-like humanoid, carrying a scepter-like weapon. The other was a lizard-like creature with four legs and a tail that looked like a serrated blade.

"What the hell are those?" Alex dashed to stand between Megan and the creatures. I followed his lead and stood beside him. Suddenly, the fly began to speak.

"Greetingsss, humansss," it hissed. He lifted his hands like the pope greeting his followers. "Today isss the end of this world asss you know it." He let out a small cackle. "Our Lord and Massster—Satan—has decided it is time to wage his war and ssseize the earth asss hisss own." The serpent raised its tail and lashed it down at a kid who was trying to run for help. It pierced his back, and he collapsed, lifeless. The serpent's tail glowed for a second before he set it back down. Another student, standing close, let out a scream and fainted. The fly continued on, "Now that you know essscape is futile, let me tell you—not all isss bad. You humansss will not sssuffer long. Your sssouls have been chosen to become the key to open the door for my massster." I noticed one of the cheerleaders letting out a soft sob. Thinking on my feet, I leaned closer to Alex.

"I'm gonna buy you some time," I whispered.

"What are you talking about?" he whispered back. "Don't be an idiot!"

"It's okay." I reached over slowly and gave his hand a squeeze. "When you see the opening, take Megan and get the hell out of here."

"Dude, don't!" He tried to reason. I mouthed "protect them" to him, and he stopped and nodded.

"It'll be okay…somehow." I gave his hand another squeeze before taking a deep breath and breaking away from the cluster. I took a step forward.

"Well, it looksss like one of the humansss chose to go first," the fly said as he turned to watch me approach. As I got close, I noticed Alex moving toward Megan out of the corner of my eye.

"Sssince you are volunteering," the creature continued, "I will be the one to take your sssoul." I held my breath from the terrible stench that wafted from what I guessed was his mouth. I heard gasps as he raised his scepter in the air. "Believe me, human, thisss is an honor." He hurled it down aiming for my head. At the very last moment, I sidestepped out of the way. Acting quickly, I grabbed the sides of the scepter and kicked away from the fly. The scepter came with me as I rolled away from the fly. The lizard lashed its tail at me, and I deflected it using the scepter.

"Everyone, this is our chance. Let's go!" Alex shouted and started ushering our fellow classmates toward the cars.

"Foolish, human, your painful death will be in vain!" The fly squawked, lifting himself off the ground to dart at me. I dodged and glanced and saw that everyone, except Alex and Megan, had made it to their cars. The flying beast had noticed this too.

"No one else shall leave this place!" It nodded, and the lizard launched its tail at me. I prepared to deflect when it made a sudden turn and caught my hand. Out of pain, I opened my grip, and the scepter went flying.

"*Sam!*" I heard Alex cry as the tail came propelling back, stabbing me through the abdomen. I couldn't even scream or cry. I felt my strength leaving me. The lizard then flung me onto the lake. As I sank below the surface, I noticed Alex and Megan surrounded by a sea of red creatures. I slowly lost consciousness.

Chapter Two

I awoke with a start, feeling my abdomen for a puncture wound only to come up empty-handed.

"What the hell?" I yelled, standing up and looking again for a gash where I was stabbed. "What's going on?"

That's when I observed that all I could see around me was white. I couldn't even perceive where the ground was.

"Where am I?" I screamed and heard it echoed. I tried to move, but it felt like I was moving in slow-motion, as though I was scurrying through mud. I ran around for a while and still, nothing. "Am I...dead?"

"More like in a comatose state." I spun around looking for the voice that said that. As I looked up, I noticed an orb of darkness descended and stopped in front of me. "You are currently inside the lake," it continued. "I am using my powers to keep you alive. You have a choice to make: I could use the rest of my power to protect your soul and send it to your heaven. In doing so, we both shall perish."

"I'll be with my family again," I smiled. It faded quickly when the darkness revealed an image of Alex surrounded by red creatures, trying to protect Megan and himself from them.

The second option came from the darkness.

"You may also choose to save your friend."

"How?" I asked as I saw the panic in Alex's eyes. He broke through a pack of them, only to have another group appear and cut them off.

"My physical body has long been destroyed, but if you surrender your body to me, I promise to save your friend. No harm will come to him." The image faded away.

Fear crept into me.

"Surrender my body?"

"Let us make a pact. Your soul will remain within your body, much like I was." I looked down and noticed that my birthmark was missing. "In return, I shall use my power to destroy the demons there and save your friend."

"So...I die either way?" I asked, confused.

"No! If you die, I die." I sensed irritation in its voice. "Your soul will be in a deep slumber, like I have been your entire life." I was wide-eyed at the sudden realization.

"So you've been within me the whole time?" I thought about the fits of foul temper I used to have and how my birthmark used to radiate heat when I had those.

"Yes, your birthmark is proof that I existed," it replied as though it was reading my mind.

"Now, time is running out for your friend. You need to make a decision."

I quickly ran my choices through my mind. It was then that I felt a feeling of dread in my chest; I knew Alex's time was running out.

"Let's do it," I said, stepping closer to the orb. "I'd never forgive myself for being selfish. My friend needs you. How do we do this?" I gulped, staring straight into the ceaseless cloud of darkness emanating from the sphere.

"Simple," the voice replied, "just reach into my sphere, and I'll take care of the rest."

"Okay." I stepped forward and nodded. "You better save Alex." I thrusted my hand into the sphere and felt the intense heat.

"The pact has been forged," the voice declared. "Tiamat lives again!"

13

Suddenly the sphere expanded and engulfed me. I thought of my family and of Alex. I felt I was losing control of my body. With a sudden rush, I felt myself flying out of the water and hovering. I let out a shriek as the demon commanders turned toward me.

"*Imposssible!*" screamed the fly creature. "Dragonsss aren't supposed to involve themselvesss in this dimension. Balzac, take care of things here," he ordered the lizard that had stabbed me.

"I've got to report to Lucifer." With that, the fly opened a portal and walked through it. The minions had backed Alex and Megan into a corner while I flung myself forward and landed between them.

"What the hell is that?" I heard Meagan shout out in fear as I unleashed a torrent of fire onto the minion horde, killing them all in a single blast. The serpent screamed out in frustration and charged at us from the beach.

"Whatever it is, it's helping us," Alex said as I felt myself flying at the serpent and spewing flames at it. The serpent whipped its tail at me. The beast within me, Tiamat, caught the tail in its talons and instantly took off high into the sky, carrying Balzac along as it cried out in shock. Tiamat flew in a circle, gaining momentum, before letting go of Balzac, sending him plummeting to the ground at great speed. The beast flew after Balzac. When he hit the ground, I could feel Tiamat unleashing another shot of flames at him. When the smoke cleared, I spotted Balzac's lifeless body disintegrating into nothingness. Satisfied, Tiamat landed in front of Alex and Megan.

"Thank you," Alex said, stepping toward me. I felt joy exuding from Tiamat.

"Get away from that monster, Alex!" I heard Megan shout out in fear. "It single-handedly killed those creatures. It's too dangerous." When she said that, I let my annoyance show on my face. Suddenly, I was blinded by red rage; I felt pure anger and bloodlust from Tiamat as he reared back and prepared to kill Megan.

"Stop it!" I heard Alex shout out before the anger consuming me began to fade. Tiamat stood up and stared at Alex. Tiamat let out a roar, and I felt his anger rising again. I sensed him preparing to kill them both and opened my eyes in the darkness.

"You promised!" I cried out. "Now stop it."

"That was before he stood in my way," it answered as the darkness turned red, and Tiamat's anger swelled up.

"Sam, I know you're in there somewhere. You need to fight this. You can win!" Alex shouted.

"That's Sam?" Megan cried out. "There's no way!"

"I don't know how it is or how I know, but I do," Alex answered as he stepped within an arm's distance.

"Your friend is brave and smart," said Tiamat as his anger continued to escalate. "But it ends now!" he reared up to attack. Just before the attack could land Alex rushed in and hugged him.

"I won't let you hurt him!" I shouted out and noticed a white beam radiating from my body. Over the blinding light, I heard Tiamat shrieking out in pain. When the light faded out, I found myself standing at the lake again with Alex's arms around me. My legs buckled, and I fell into his arms.

"Welcome back," Alex said as we stood there.

"Welcome back? Welcome back?" Megan fumed. "Is that all you have to say after that *monster* tried to kill me?"

"He saved us though." Alex shrugged as I tried to stay conscious. "Seriously though, what was that about? How and what did you transform into?"

"I don't really know how to explain," I said. "I don't really understand it myself." Sitting down on the grass with Alex's help.

"Well, what do you know?" asked Alex, sitting down next to me. I looked at Megan and then back at him. He noticed and knew what I was thinking. "Megan, why don't you go back home, and I'll call you later?" he asked gently.

"And leave you with *monster-boy* here?" she spat. "I don't think so."

"Don't call him a monster!" Alex screamed at her. He walked up to her to argue. "Besides, he's not going to hurt me even if he changes again," he reasoned. "You saw him hesitate when I stepped between him and you. I'll be fine."

"Even still...," Megan argued, "if those things come back—"

Alex placed his hand on her shoulder. "They won't, at least for now. You heard that fly. This is the actual apocalypse they are trying to start. Now that they know something can fight back against them, they are going to strategize. Go home, warn your family if they listen. You are needed there." He locked eyes with her. "I promise I'll be safe, and I'll call you the second we get home and get a grasp on what's going on."

"You better call before the end of the day." She glared at me before stomping off to Alex's car and pulling out.

"Sorry," I muttered, curling into a ball.

"For what?" He sat down beside me.

"Causing yet another rift between you and Megan," I said, rocking gently.

"A rift that wouldn't have even happened if you hadn't saved us," he tried to reassure me and tapped my shoulder to get my attention. "Now, spill. What was all that about?"

"I don't know everything, but here's what I do know…" I proceeded to tell him about waking up in a comatose state, the white around me, the dark mass, the voice, the pact, and everything I had experienced while the dragon controlled me.

"So this…thing—" he started to sum up.

"Tiamat," I corrected.

"Right," he agreed. "So, Tiamat has always been inside of you?"

"According to him anyway." I shrugged.

"And to save me, you sold your soul to him?" he questioned.

"Not exactly—more like my body. When he's in control of it, my soul just lays dormant," I clarified before being smacked in the back of the head.

"Idiot!" he belted out.

"What was that for?" I rubbed my head.

"You could have been in peace!" he fumed. "You could have been with our families again, in peace, if you had abandoned me!"

"I…I…," I stammered.

"All hell is literally about to be unleashed, and you could have avoided it if you just let…" He trailed off, and his eyes welling up a bit.

"If I would have just what?" I asked, standing up to lock eyes with him. "Sacrificed you?" I raised my voice in irritation. "How could I have lived in peace knowing that your soul was suffering to build some portal to hell?" Tears began streaming freely down my face. "You know how much you mean to me, dude. I would do it all over again in a heartbeat."

"I'm sorry. You're right." He stood up and gave me a quick hug. "I mean, what's done is done, right? We will figure this out together." He grabbed my hand and pointed at the birthmark that came back. "First question. How did you regain control of your body?"

"I think because he was going to break the pact," I said, thinking out loud.

"What do you mean? He saved Megan and me," Alex replied. "I don't think he's evil."

"I never said that, and I honestly believe he's not evil. I sensed good emotions too," I explained. "But right after he had saved you, Megan called him a monster. I myself felt annoyance, and I think he fed off that emotion coming from me. After that, all I had felt around me was pure bloodlust. When he was willing to hurt you, I felt energized and was able to break through."

"Well, that would explain it," Alex agreed. "So the next question is, what's the next move?"

"How disappointing." Alex and I jolted at the sudden voice. "I come all this way and risk exposure to see a dragon, and all I find is a mortal and the dragon's weak vessel." A humanoid with black wings shimmered into view in front of us. I stepped between Alex and the mysterious figure.

"I'll show you a weak vessel," I challenged, taking on a defensive stance.

He raised his hands in innocence. "Easy there! I come in peace. I apologize for offending you, oh mighty vessel." He bowed to me in mockery. "I go by the name Loki."

I eased up. "So why are you here?" I asked, standing still between him and Alex.

"I've known of Lucifer's plan for a long time, and I've been aiding humans with research, hoping they could defend themselves when the time comes," he explained. "I thought all had been in vain, but when Beelzebub returned and spoke of a dragon, I knew someone must have succeeded."

"Beelzebub?" Alex questioned.

"That annoying suck-up of Lucifer's." Loki fumed and took a deep breath. "He is the one who held the scepter and had a lizard pet that your dragon slayed."

"He looked like a fly?" I asked, already knowing the answer.

"A fly?" Loki asked before breaking up in a laugh. "He would be pissed if he had heard you call him that. He is already pissed you killed his pet."

"All right, that explains some of what happened, but why are you still here? Your dragon is gone," I said.

"Not gone," Loki grinned. "Hibernating. You are a special child. Your body has two souls. One that is human—yourself. And the other is the member of the dark dragon clan from another universe—Tiamat. Just because the pact was broken doesn't mean he's out of your body." Loki stretched out his hand, and a shimmering black crystal appeared in his hand. He turned his palms, and the crystal floated over to me. When it reached me, the crystal exploded, leaving a necklace with a black crystal in the center. "Consider this a gift." The necklace lowered itself into my hands.

"What is it?" I asked. The necklace seemed to be screaming for me to put it around my neck.

"The legendary dragon crystal," Loki informed. "Well, a part of it anyway. Legend has it that it used to be translucent with a radiant shine. When the dragon tribes waged battle, the crystal had broken in two—light and shadow."

"Dragons don't exist!" Alex shouted out, trying to remain calm.

"Then how do you explain what had happened to your friend?" Loki answered like he was talking to a small child.

"I...I..." Alex searched for the answer.

"You are, in a certain sense, right though. Dragons usually don't exist here on this plane." He threw his hand out, and a portal appeared. "However, I have the power to walk between those planes and bring others with me. Well, their souls anyway."

Alex started to get angry. "So you put that thing in Sam?"

"I did no such thing," Loki grinned slyly. "All I did was provide the dragon soul. Humans did the rest."

"You're the cause of all this?" Alex stepped out from behind me.

"No, he's not," I answered, and Alex turned to stare at me.

"But...," he struggled for words.

"He actually gave humans a fighting chance," I reasoned. "This attack was going to happen eventually."

"If you believe he is trying to help"—Alex stared at Loki as he said this, searching for a reaction—"My next question is, who are the humans you had given Tiamat's soul to?"

"Interesting you asked." Loki laughed a little. "I gave it to—" Suddenly the police turned up into the lot with their sirens blaring. "It seems I've overstayed my welcome. Another time perhaps." With that, Loki shimmered out.

"Are you, boys, all right?" asked one of the officers as he came up to us. The others began to comb the area for demons and dead bodies. Alex and I only nodded. "Good," he continued. "We heard stories about monsters in the area, but all I see is one dead body and you two. We need you both to come in for questioning now."

I nodded at Alex, clutching the necklace Loki gave me as we walked to the officer's squad car.

Chapter Three

"This is bull!" Alex belted as he paced the cell we were in. I lay back in the bed, tossing the necklace repeatedly in the air. "Calm down, man, getting upset won't get us out any quicker," I reasoned.

"How are you so calm?" he snapped. "They know we didn't do anything, and yet we're still locked up."

"Look, they just don't know what to think right now." I sat up and looked him in the eye. "Besides, if I'm in here, I know I won't hurt anyone innocent. You heard Loki, Tiamat is still alive but just sleeping." I clutched the necklace again.

"What are you going to do about that?" Alex asked, pointing at the necklace.

I sighed. "I think I'm going to try and put it on while we are in here."

"But we don't know Loki's true intentions," he panicked. "What if you lose yourself when you put it on?"

"Then you will either kill me or bring me back around," I declared. "I don't think that's Loki's plan. Yes, I think he has a hidden agenda, and we are just pawns. However, I don't think it is turning me into public enemy number one. At least, not yet." I closed my eyes, took a deep breath, and put the necklace on.

"Well?" Alex asked after a moment of silence.

"Well, nothing, I guess." I looked at the black crystal and sighed. "I don't think it did anything. I don't feel any different. Still me in here." I tapped my head, and Alex just kind of shrugged.

I wouldn't say that it did nothing, a voice boomed.

"Did you say something?" I asked Alex. He only shook his head.

I never thought a human would be able to take back over and push me back into the dark recesses of your body. I'm impressed. It sounded condescending this time.

"Tell me you at least heard that," I pleaded with Alex.

"Dude, what's going on?" He walked up and rested his hand on my shoulder. "You're freaking me out."

I shook his hand off and sat on the cell bed. "I think I can hear Tiamat."

Tiamat roared with laughter. *About time you connected the dots.*

What the hell did I get involved in? I thought, leaning back and closing my eyes.

You made a pact with a dragon instead of dying—that's what. Tiamat laughed again.

So you can hear my thoughts? I asked internally.

Looks like it. Either the shard of dragon crystal allows it, or the fact that I controlled your body is causing it. Either way, I hear you loud and clear, he explained.

"Dude, answer me!" I snapped back as Alex shook me. "What's going on?"

"Well, somehow I can communicate with Tiamat now," I replied.

"So, you're saying…" Alex's body froze midsentence.

I waved my hand in front of his face. "Alex?"

"Glad to hear the dragon is awake." I spun around to see Loki walk into the room.

"What's going on?" I asked. "Why is Alex frozen?"

"Not just him," Loki answered. "I froze time to get you out of here. Beelzebub was ordered to kill you at any cost. They had used a dragon's weed to pinpoint you at the jail. He's sending another underling to kill you. This one is fast, and you're not ready." He opened the cell door.

"What about Alex?" I asked, and Loki shook his head.

"If I try to take him, time will unfreeze, and you both will perish," Loki tried to reason. "I'm sorry, but you need to leave him. The demon should just go after the dragon."

"No way." I broke free from his grip. "I'm not leaving him."

"Look, your destiny is to impede the apocalypse, and sacrifices must be made!" He pulled me again, but I grabbed on to the prison bars to hold my ground.

"Not him!" I said, holding the bars with all my might.

"Time's almost up, you stubborn human," Loki rasped. "Time will soon unfreeze, and you will both die."

Let me out, I'll kill any demon! Tiamat yelled.

Last time, you, lost control, I reminded him.

The crystal will help keep my sanity. Trust me...you die, I die. Remember? he pleaded.

All right! I gave in and kicked Loki away. "Take Alex and get out of here undetected," I ordered Loki. "Tiamat is sure he can take him on." I could see the anger in Loki's eyes. "Make sure Alex gets home. If anything happens, I won't hold Tiamat back from eating you for supper."

"Say I listen," Loki spat, "how do you think I can get out undetected with him? I don't have destructive powers. All I have is passive."

Leave that to me, Tiamat stated. I relayed this to Loki just as we heard screaming and gunfire. Alex unfroze as well.

All right, let's do this. I nodded. *How though? Last time, I formed a pack and touched the dark mass while I was comatose.*

Use the crystal, Tiamat instructed. *Believe in its power.*

I closed my eyes and wished on the crystal, ignoring Alex's questions. *Please work. I need to protect my loved ones. Let Tiamat and I switch again.* I felt a gust of wind encircle me before a sensation of falling. When the gust stopped, I was back, sensing my body without control, and Tiamat was in front of Alex and Loki. Tiamat flew into the window of the cell and knocked it out. Loki grabbed Alex and, before Alex could object, jumped out the open window to flee. *Now to take care of this demon.* Tiamat unleashed his fire on the bars and stepped through as they crumbled. He busted through to the entrance of the station. A slender demon stood erect on top of the last dying policeman. Its long silver hair seemed to emit a dull-light glow as it crouched down and lashed out its tongue, wrapping it around the officer's neck. As the officer breathed his last, the demon's tongue ingested a white light emanating from him.

"Looks like the mighty dragon finally showed up," it said in a feminine voice. Tiamat unleashed his flames at it, but she quickly dodged out of the way. "Didn't anyone tell you it's not polite to hit a lady?" Like lightning, she maneuvered next to Tiamat and stabbed his side. He roared in pain. "So the Dragon's Bane Dagger is fatal to dragons." She laughed gleefully. "Hell will rejoice my name. They will speak of how the mighty Tiamat was defeated by the great Asura!" she shouted triumphantly. Tiamat hurled a weak fire at her as he collapsed to the ground.

I'm sorry I was cocky, Tiamat apologized as I felt his soul getting weaker.

Take it out of you! I urged.

Impossible. Dragons Bane is fatal. Even if I remove it, the damage is done. He sounded defeated.

It's not to humans though, right? I pondered. *Give me back control. I'll pull it out and give you control once you get your strength back,* I suggested.

Asura will kill you before I recover, he shot back. *It's over.*

Tiamat, stay with me! I shouted. *I've got an idea.*

Speak fast then. I can't hold out much longer. Distance grew between his thoughts.

Pull your soul into the crystal, I ordered.

What? he asked, confused.

I know you can feel the crystal if I can, I explained. *It's almost like another soul in here. Give me back control, but you aim for the crystal. I'll take it from there.*

*But Asura...*he hesitated.

If we do nothing, you die, then I die, I pleaded. *Trust me.*

Very well, he relented. *You trusted me again. I will trust you, vessel.*

I felt that same falling sensation and woke up just in time to see Asura bringing her sword down. I rolled out of the way and stood up, clutching the side where the dagger was sticking out.

"You must be the human vessel," she said snidely. "Sorry about your dragon's untimely demise."

"Tiamat's not de"—I pulled the dagger out as I spoke—"dead!"

"Wishful thinking," Asura retorted. "I'll make your death a fast one." She walked slowly toward me before picking up her speed. I threw the dagger at her, causing her to stop and dodge. "Foolish human!" she hissed. "You wanna play first? Let's play."

"Sounds good to me," I countered as I prayed to the crystal. I noticed her stop dead in her tracks, and I looked down to see the crystal glowing.

"What are you trying at, human? What is that?" She seemed entranced by the dark light.

"A new hope." I smiled as the crystal's dark pulsation engulfed me. I was suddenly face-to-face with Tiamat.

"A new power is born!" a voice called out, and Tiamat and I looked up into the darkness above. "Human and dragon working together to attain greater heights. Young One, call it out, embrace the power of darkness and save your world." I exchanged a glance with Tiamat, and he looked at me and nodded. I stood back and let the words flow through me. They came as naturally as though I had always said them.

"Power of Darkness!" I held my right hand over the crystal, bringing my left hand over it. "Dual"—my hands were immersed in darkness; I threw them both to the side—"*Soul!*" I felt Tiamat fly into me. When he struck me, I cried out in excruciating pain. I could feel Tiamat's pain as well. Then, in seconds, the pain was over. The darkness around us cleared, and I stood staring at Asura again; only this time, it was my turn to smirk. I felt sheer power flowing through me.

"What the hell are you?" Asura cried out and charged at me in full-speed. I followed her movements with ease, sidestepping and maneuvering a roundhouse kick, sending her flying back. "Where did the vessel go?" she cried.

"I am Sam and Tiamat," I responded as she pulled out her sword and charged at me again. Without breaking a sweat, I stepped to the side and whipped a roundhouse on her back. "We are one," I yelled. She shrieked and came swinging her sword violently.

"No human is faster than me," she said before beginning to spin like a tornado, and the blade appeared to be a blur. Asura began to cackle. "You fought valiantly human, but prepare to die."

"Enjoy your final laugh, Asura," I shouted back. "I told you I'm not human." I leaped up and latched on to a light attached to a pillar untouched by the flames. She stopped spinning and looked up. "I am a hybrid—with the cunningness of a human"—I spotted the dragon's bane dagger and jumped at it—"and the powers of a dark dragon." I grasped the dagger, ignoring the stinging sensation in my hand. I appeared right behind a shocked Asura, who was trying hard to follow my movements. "I am a dragon ninja," I jeered, stabbing her in the heart. She let out a wild scream before turning to stone and disintegrating along with the dagger. "Well, that was an odd way to die," I chuckled. I heard the fire department pull up and looked around at the dead bodies. *I better not stick around.* I bolted back to the cell and leaped out the same exit Loki had used.

You think, Tiamat chuckled as I hit the ground and bolted home before anyone could spot me. I leaped over the privacy fence and knocked on the back door. I noticed a pair of eyes peeking through the blinds.

"It's just me, Alex," I said.

Alex opened the door. "What the hell happened to you?" Alex asked as I stepped in.

"I reached an understanding with Tiamat," I laughed, and he scrunched up his face in confusion. I noticed that the house was quiet. "I figured Loki would bail once you were home, but where's Megan?"

"After much debate, I persuaded her to go stay with her parents," he explained. "With her dad being mayor, I figured she would be much safer with them rather than with me."

"Makes sense." I nodded. "You should go too."

"Not happening," he cried out. "I'm not going anywhere."

"Look at me!" I roared, making him flinch. "I'm the making of some weird experiment, and I'm going to be in constant danger." I ceased hoping that would be enough to get him going.

"All I see is my best friend," he replied calmly, "and we are going to get through this…together." He tried to place his hand on my shoulder but had to remove it quickly for the heat I was emitting. "The first step is to find whoever Loki gave Tiamat's spirit to. Is there anything you can do about your appearance?"

I looked at myself in the mirror in the hallway. My hair was pitch-black and was now at shoulder length. My eyes were pitch-black as well, and my skin had scales that reflected. My muscles were much more prominent. I turned to look at my back; I noticed a spot for wings, but they weren't there yet. "What? It freaks you out?" I spat out.

"No, but the investigation will be a whole lot easier if you didn't look like a beast yourself," he explained. "Not to mention that I would like to be able to console my best friend without getting a third-degree burn." He chuckled, still waving his hand from touching my shoulder.

"There's something I can try." I brought my hand to my chest and closed my eyes. I prayed to the crystal to restore me. Instantly, I felt a gust of cold wind; I also felt myself sweating as though I had just broken a fever. I suddenly felt weak and fell forward. I sensed myself get caught, and when I opened my eyes, I found Alex looking down at me. "This is the second time you caught me." I smiled.

"I wouldn't have to if someone quit pushing themselves to the brink of death." He smiled back

"At least this time, I didn't *actually* die." I got on my feet with his help and reached out to check on Tiamat. *You still with us man?*

For better or worse, Tiamat replied.

"So what's the plan?" I asked Alex, figuring he had something in mind.

"We start by looking at your family's history around the time you were born," he answered while walking toward the basement.

"Why?" I asked, rushing to catch up.

"Think about it," he started as he grabbed a box full of photo albums. "Loki said he was helping someone, right?" He flipped through one before tossing it aside. "And Tiamat said your birthmark is proof he has always been in you, right?" He threw another book aside after flipping through it.

"So?"

"So that means, at some point before you were born, some-one put Tiamat into you." He flipped through another, and stopped, placing his finger on one. "We were both born the same day, so luck-ily I have photos that weren't destroyed by the fire." He tapped on the picture. "I suggest we start our investigation here."

"Okay. I get your point, but we weren't born in a hospital, remember? I know my mom wasn't the most forthcoming, and all I ever got was that '*work* took *care* of her,'" I said, holding my fingers up in air quotes. "So I don't know where 'work' is."

"Well, I know both our moms worked at the same place," he explained. "I know Dad said it was some government job," he added. "I'm hoping these baby photos will hold some clue." He handed me another album. "Look through these and see if anything catches your eye."

I grabbed the album and took my seat next to him. A rush of memories passed through my mind as I flipped through the pages. "Man, it's been a long time since I've seen these pictures," I said as I smiled at a picture of Alex with a broken arm and me signing the cast. I had just learned how to write my name then. "We really have been through a lot together, huh?" I flipped to another picture of us camping out in my backyard because my mom wouldn't let us go camping for real.

"Yeah, we have, man." He laughed at a picture he flipped to. "Here's a picture of us after we got sent home from school when we started a food fight."

"Hey, as I recall, you started it when Tony picked on me in the lunchroom. I just helped you finish it." I chuckled and threw a pillow at him, striking his head. I brushed my shoulder a couple of times. "Still got it," I said before we both broke out in a laugh for a minute.

"There are literally hundreds of pictures here," Alex said, pulling the two of us back on track. "There has to be some clue if we keep looking."

"I agree." I flipped to a picture of our moms holding us side by side. "This must have been taken right after we were born." I took it out and walked over to him. "Look at how young our moms were."

"Damn, that was a long time ago," he said, grabbing hold of the photograph. "The question is, where was this taken? I don't see any clue in the room."

I looked at the picture, and my eyes grew wide. "Isn't that a Big Bobs Burgers sign if you look through the window?" I asked.

"Yeah, so?" He didn't get why I was excited. "There are at least ten of those around town."

"*Today*, yes, that's the case." I smiled, and he caught on.

He began connecting the dots. "There was only one when we were born. That means…"

"Yup," I smiled. "We were born around that old Bobs that was recently demolished."

"What's around there anyway?"

"That's not the correct question," I replied. "It should be 'what *was* around there?'" He glared at me. "I don't know the answer to either."

"At least it's a lead though," he lashed out at me trying to be optimistic. "So now we come up with a plan."

"The plan is, tomorrow, I'm going to go to the old site with the picture and try to see if I can find where it was taken."

"So, tomorrow afternoon we—" Alex started.

"No, I'm going in the morning. I figure it will take all day." I interjected, shaking my head

"But classes start tomorrow." He protested.

"Not for me." I sat down again after handing the book back. "Look, we don't even know *if* there will be school tomorrow, and if there is, I'm willing to bet it will be flooded with security."

"You make that sound like a bad thing." Alex sounded startled.

"It is…for two reasons." I said, leaning closer to him. "One is, if Megan spills the beans on what happened at the lake, I doubt I'll be able to even reach the front door. Second, I doubt if guns even work on these things. You saw it for yourself—these things kill, and they kill fast. If you could have seen the blood bath at the station." I shivered slightly.

"That's why you need to be there," he tried to reason. "You *can* do something against them. And don't worry about Megan. I'll make sure she stays quiet."

"You're not with her constantly, man. For all you know, she could be telling her dad now." He scowled at me as I gave my rebuttal. "Look, I know you trust her, and that's fine. This is *my* secret though, and she *hates* me."

"She doesn't hate you, man," he said quietly.

"You and I both know that's a lie," I said. "The only reason she puts up with me is because she is afraid if she didn't, you would leave her." I could see the pain in his eyes, so I changed the subject. "But Megan's drama aside, when Loki froze time, he said that they had tracked me with something. He called it dragons weed."

"Tracked you?"

"Whatever Dragon's Weed is, I'm guessing it pinpoints the locations of dragons, and since I have one in me…" I paused, hoping he would finish.

"There is nothing stopping them from doing it again. I see." He grasped my point.

"Right now, they are after me. To minimize exposure and protect the general population, I think it's best if I avoid large crowds." I hoped he wouldn't fight me anymore on this.

"All right. So for now, school is a no-go for us." He stood up and dusted himself off. "We will leave in the morning then."

"You should come and meet up with me after," I pleaded and was met with a "hell no" stare. "There's no way to talk you into going ahead to class, is there?" He shook his head, and I sighed in defeat. "All right, we go to Bob's tomorrow morning then."

Chapter Four

I was jolted awake by my alarm. I looked at the clock, and it read 5:30 AM. As quickly and quietly as I could, I got dressed and grabbed the photo. I peeked into Alex's room as I passed and saw him sleeping peacefully. I hurried to my car and pulled out of the driveway, driving downtown. *Sorry Alex, but I can't put you in anymore danger than I already have.* I sighed watching the sun rising.

I thought you and Alex were going together today? Tiamat asked me.

I just agreed to that, so we wouldn't fight, I explained. *I have a bad feeling the demons are going to attack me today, and I don't want to risk his life, not to mention, digging into our unknown past. Who knows what skeletons I'll find.*

You think too much, human, Tiamat laughed. *We dragons like to run on pure instinct. Thought tends to lead to conflict.*

Is that how the dragon crystal split? I asked. *And thought isn't all that bad. Pure instinct almost got you killed by Asura.*

That wasn't pure instinct. I was just careless, he huffed.

Right, I laughed at his childlike pouting.

The dragon crystal split before my time though, vessel, he admitted. *I do not know the exact cause of how the dark shard and light shard came to be.*

I do have a name, you know. I threw out to him.

"Man, the silence here is deafening." Alex popped his head up from my backseat, and I jumped and swerved from the shock. He grabbed my headrest to keep himself from flying around. Laughing, he climbed into the front seat.

"Jesus Christ, Alex, you almost gave me a heart attack!" I exclaimed and smacked his stomach as he kept laughing. I tried to get my heartbeat back to normal.

"That's for trying to ditch me," he said, calming down.

"I...just...I...," I stammered for words.

"It's cool. I get it." He put his feet up on the dashboard. "I'd probably do the same thing if the situation was reversed." We sat in silence for a while as I drove. Finally, he put his feet down and turned the radio on. "I can't take it anymore, dude. It's too quiet." An emergency broadcast came over the radio.

"Ladies and gentlemen, the mayor of our fine city has called for an emergency broadcast in order to speak to you all in light of recent events," the announcer spoke. "Here he is, Mayor Andrew Lokai."

"Thank you, John," the mayor came on. "People of Newson, as you are all aware, the police department was attacked last night."

"The rumor is its demons," John piped up.

"That would be true, John," Andrew confirmed. "However, I have it on good authority that it's not just demons. Our fair city is smack dab in the middle of a war between demons and dragons." I slammed my fist on the steering wheel when he said that; Alex flinched at that, but he stayed quiet. "However, fear not. I have contacted DC, and they have sent in help. We will carry on with our normal lives and show these monsters we are not afraid. The military is placing troops at schools and throughout the city to engage the enemy if they show themselves. Stand tall and stay proud, people. We will survive this!" The radio switched from the broadcast to music. Then I zoned out to talk to Tiamat.

Really glad I'm a person who doesn't just run off emotion, I said

Why is that? Tiamat questioned.

Because if I ran on impulse, I would jump out of this car and go rip the mayor and his daughter's throats out! I screamed internally. *We are not the bad guys. Does he have any idea how many more, including*

his daughter, would be dead right now and the demons that would be running loose?

"Sam, talk to me." Alex tried to get my attention.

Humans are cowardly creatures, saying and doing what it takes to get to the top and stay there, Tiamat said as my anger seethed.

"Sam!" Alex shouted, and I jumped slightly. "Don't lock up on me, dude. Talk to me!"

"I can't defend them." I took a deep breath, and my anger subsided. I pulled over to collect my thoughts. "I can't defend them," I sighed, turning off the motor and resting my head on my hands against the steering wheel.

"What?" Alex asked, caught off guard by everything.

"Everyone is treating me like a villain in this," I spoke through my arms. "All I wanted to do was to protect people, especially you, and they blame me for it. If it wasn't for them, putting Tiamat in me—"

"Dude, not everyone thinks you're the villain," Alex interrupted.

"You don't count," I said, sitting up to look at him with tears in my eyes.

"That hurts." He smiled, acting as though I shot him.

"You know what I mean." Tears started to flow, and I didn't hide them. "I just don't know how to bring myself to fight for people who are going to hate and even try to kill me. With Megan spilling the beans, it may not be wise to even go home now." I leaned back against my seat and covered my eyes, taking deep breaths to calm down.

"Dude, it'll work out." He pulled out his phone. "I'm going to find out exactly what she had told her dad."

"Don't," I pleaded. "I don't think I can take it."

"I'm doing it." He looked me in the eyes. "I need to know if you are in danger of going home. I need to know if we are running away."

"But Megan…" I began.

"I was thinking about what you had said last night." He finished sending his text and placed his hand on my knee. "You were right about one thing: she doesn't want to find out the answer if I have to choose between the two of you." He smiled at me. "Now,

take a deep breath, calm down, and let's find out who did this to us."
I nodded, leaning forward and started the car. By now, the sun was
mostly up, and I didn't even bother turning the headlights back on.
My mind began to swirl with thoughts of what lay ahead—all the
what ifs. What if we find nothing? What if they shoot first and we die
there? What if we find out our families were hiding all this from us?

"I hope we don't regret this," I said as we pulled into the abandoned lot. I noticed a young girl crouched in the rubble.

"Isn't that Harmony from school?" Alex asked.

"Who?" I turned to him and back to look at her.

"Harmony, the girl who is pretty much a guarantee for valedic-
torian," he answered. "Harmony Meadows, I think."

"I think you're right." I agreed, watching as she scooped up
some dirt and filled it in a container. "It looks like she's taking soil
samples. But why?" We were startled when she screamed in terror
and jumped back. The ground began to swirl as though a plug had
been pulled. Then, out of the center, demons similar to the horde
that had trapped Alex and Megan hopped out one after another. We
opened the doors and bolted for them. "Alex, get Harmony some-
place safe. I'll deal with these guys," I ordered.

"Will do. Stay safe, man!"

All right, Tiamat, let's do this! I brought my right hand to my
chest as I ran. "Power of Darkness!" I brought my left hand to join
my right. "Dual…" Then, bringing both my arms to my side, I
yelled, "Soul!" In a flash, I transformed into the ninja again. I jumped
between Harmony and a horde demon, catching its talon and causing it to shriek in surprise. I noticed the black scales on my hand
seemed to pull the light in while I fought. I was pitch black all over.
I kicked it back and glanced back to see Alex ushering Harmony
away. *Any idea how to kill these things?* I asked, sending another flying
back, keeping them from going after Alex who was ducked inside a
building. *I have no weapons.*

This is all new to me too, vessel, he replied. *Have faith in the
crystal though. It would not have left you unarmed.* I flipped back to
put a gap between me and the horde. I brought my right hand to my
chest and concentrated on the crystal. I looked down and noticed

a flat black circle between my index and middle finger. One of the hordes ran after me, and I flung the circle at him. It struck its chest and exploded, causing it to fall and disintegrate.

Awesome! Exploding shurikens, I ran a big circle around the hoard, darting shurikens at them and taking them out one by one. When the last one fell, I tensed up, waiting for something to appear. When nothing did, I relaxed and looked around. *That was random. Why just send horde demons?* I asked Tiamat. *If they were planning an attack, where is the big guy?*

Maybe they are distracting us while something else is happening, He suggested. *It may be possible they didn't know we were here, and the girl may have been the target?*

But they can track us, I interjected. *Loki let us in on that little secret.*

"Sam!" I jumped as my thoughts were interrupted. Alex was at the entrance of a building waving me down. "You got to see this!" he exclaimed. I leaped over to him in a single jump. "Show off," he laughed.

"Now that your girlfriend has announced to half the world who I am," I smirked as he took half a step back.

"Dude, you're on fire, remember?" He fanned himself.

"Sorry." I concentrated and turned back to human. Swaying from the sudden energy drop, he held my shoulder to steady me. I shook my head to clear the fog way. "Hey, hey, there is a bright side," I laughed. "I didn't nearly pass out this time. So what did you want to show me?"

"It's Harmony. She—" He was interrupted by someone clearing her throat. I spun around and noticed Harmony appearing from a side door in the building.

"Thank god, Tiamat's soul still lives," she said, motioning for us to come over. "Your two must come with me. Father will be so pleased." I glared at Alex after staring a moment at Harmony's waving form.

"Hey, I didn't say anything." He threw up his hands in innocence. "She seems to have some idea of what's going on by herself. I say we play along."

34

"But, dude, if she knows everything, who knows what we are walking into," I hesitated.

"Look, I don't like it any more than you," he whispered. "But you want to know the truth, right?" I nodded. "Then our best bet is through that door *with* Harmony."

"You're right." I relented and began walking toward her, Alex in tow. I leaned in close as we walked and added, "Stay close though. If things get dangerous in there, I want to be able to grab you and go. Deal?"

"Deal," he nodded as we reached Harmony's side

"You can relax around me, Sam. I will not harm you or Alex," Harmony said, giving me a friendly smile. "I know the truth about you, and of that 'dragon and demon war,'" she said, motioning air quotes. "What Mayor Lokai had told us about is a farce." I opened my mouth in shock. "I know the demons are truly here to cause the apocalypse to happen early, using pure souls to open the door to hell, and you are fighting against them."

"How? I mean…how?" I stammered at a loss for words.

"All will be explained, but you must follow me in silence," she said, ushering us inside and closing the door. After she bolted the door, she set what looked like a Japanese paper charm over the magnetic swipe lock.

"What is—" I started to say, but she hushed me up and motioned for me to follow. Alex and I glanced at each other before following her down the hallway. She stopped in front of the elevators. Pulling out a card from behind her school badge, she swiped it in the reader in between the elevators. Then she pulled on the reader when the light turned green, and the wall between the elevators opened up like a door, revealing a stairwell behind it. She motioned for Alex and me to go ahead. Alex and I stepped in and waited. She shut the passage and motioned for us to follow as she descended into the darkness. Alex motioned for me to go first and smirked when I flipped him off as I started down the stairs. I stopped at the bottom and reached my hand behind me for Alex; it was too dark to see. He grabbed on as he hit the last step, and I began pulling him through the darkness. I felt us walking past several metal doorways before stepping into one that slammed shut behind us. The lights came on, and I had to shield myself from the sudden brightness.

"It's okay to speak now," Harmony instructed. "Sorry for the silent journey, but we are only truly safe from demon ears here."

"Where is here?" Alex asked, stepping by my side.

"This would be a WAYCOMM lab," an older man's voice answered. I spun around to see an old man turning away from a computer and standing up. It was then that I noticed we were in an underground laboratory.

"As in WAYCOMM the government agency?" Alex asked as I tried to take everything in.

"That would be correct, Alex," the old man answered. "I am Professor James Meadows, head of the AD department. I spearheaded Project Cocoon, and both of your mothers volunteered."

"The AD department?" Alex asked.

"Project Cocoon?" I followed up.

"First things first," James turned to me. "I must thank you, Mr. Nogard, for saving my daughter. Although, I am surprised you were able to."

"What do you mean?" I asked.

"We were informed that you had chosen to fight a certain demon and had died in the process," Harmony answered.

"Yeah, well I was also supposed to be a full dragon with Tiamat in control." I crossed my arms, leaning against a counter. "That didn't last long either." I glanced at Alex who locked eyes with me.

"I know. Project Cocoon has far surpassed any expectations I had." He pushed his glasses up and ushered for me to follow him. I walked with him up to his computer. He reached into his lab coat and pulled something out. He pointed it at me and hit a button. It shot out a light, and in defense, I brought my hands up. "Relax, my boy, I just wanted a body scan." He laughed.

"Next time, warn a guy before you shoot him with something, would you?" I tried to calm down.

"Yeah, yeah, sure." He typed something onto the computer, and I saw an x-ray pop up on the monitor.

"I apologize," Harmony spoke up after she and Alex reached the computer. "Just that, ever since we had heard you had died, Father has been working nonstop to come up with a plan B."

"How did you make all this?" Alex asked, reaching out to touch a glowing tube. Harmony smacked his hand way.

"Loki," I answered for them.

"Yes and no." James got up and grabbed the glowing vial that Alex had almost touched and held it in front of him. "Loki gave us the mythical creature's soul and intel on the demons' plans. My team and I did the rest."

"So that's..." Alex began to reach for the vial again. James let him grab it.

"That's the soul of a phoenix actually," he explained, and I saw Alex's eyes shine. James turned to me and said, "When we were told you were dead, I was able to develop a set of weapons that I believe will work against them. With you leading the attack—"

"Look, that's cool and all, but I don't know what I'm doing." I cut him short. I felt as though I was beginning to implode and crumble. Alex set the vial down and walked over to me.

"You will learn what you are doing. You will lead us, and you will save mankind," James said, trying to motivate me. I think.

"Dad's right," Harmony chimed in. "After all, you saved me."

"That's not what he means," Alex said, rubbing my back to try and calm me down.

"What does he mean then?" James asked. I picked up a sudden coldness in his voice. Instinctively, I began to tense up.

"He means that—" Alex began as I stepped in between them, my arm ushering Alex to get behind me.

"I mean that I just came here to learn the truth," I answered. *What is this I'm feeling?*

"The truth?" James cracked his neck and began laughing maniacally. "The truth? You want to learn the truth?"

"Father?" Harmony cried, her voice filled with worry. "What's going on? This isn't like you."

"Experiments aren't to question, only to obey." James's eyes became black, and he began breathing deep.

"Father?" Harmony was about to cry. "Father, please calm down."

"That man is no longer your father," I responded as I transformed. "Harmony, you know this place? Take Alex and hide somewhere safe."

"But...father, please," she pleaded.

"Harmony, I'm sorry. I'll see what I can do, but get out now," I ordered. Alex grabbed her, and they both ran into the next room. I turned back to the doctor just in time to dodge a white beam coming at me. I turned behind and noticed a gaping hole where the beam had struck. I saw the professor readying the gun for another shot.

"You want the truth? Here it is." He fired a shot, and I dodged again. "Dr. James didn't know what he was getting himself into. He made a pact with Master Loki for knowledge and power and played right into our hands."

"So what exactly are you?" I bolted toward the doctor's body and grabbed the gun, struggling with him to take it.

"I am a Possessor." Before I could react, he pulled a device out of his coat and pressed a button. A green current from the device struck me and sent me flying into the wall. I crouched down, clutching my side, panting from the pain.

What are you doing vessel? Tiamat questioned. *The enemy is mortal. Finish him!*

But he's just possessed, and I want my answers. I took another hit from the bolt. I let out a scream of pain; it caused me to hit the ceiling. I struggled to stay conscious. *Man, that lightning packs a punch.*

"Why aren't you fighting back, dragon?" He laughed as he picked up the gun and aimed for my head. "I'm bored. If you're not going to fight back, I'll just finish this quickly. Goodbye, dragon." I closed my eyes and braced for the blow. Suddenly, there was a giant whoosh. "What is the meaning of this?" The possessor roared. I opened my eyes and saw him encased in a tube that had come down from the ceiling.

"Sam, are you okay?" A door opened, and Alex and Harmony came rushing back in. I transformed back to human and let Alex help me up.

"What's going on?" I asked as he continued to support me.

"You are all dead when I get out of here!" the Possessor screamed. Then he fired the Taser he had hit me with. When it ricocheted back, it hit him and knocked him out.

"Not if I can help it," Harmony said as she ran to a box with a hand scan in front and placed her hand upon it. The box opened up, and she pulled out two small pistols. She threw one to Alex, saying, "These should work against demons." She walked over to her dad's computer.

"Should?" I asked.

"Well, we haven't exactly had the chance to test half the things in here," she snapped. "I want to try to separate the possessor from my dad. If things go bad, do you think you can still fight?" I stood up straight and steadied myself. I walked up to the tube, transformed, and nodded. She typed something into the computer and hit a button. Gas started pouring into the tube. When the gas reached James, he began convulsing violently. A black figure slowly crawled out of him, hovering up when it separated. She opened up the tube, and the demon booked it toward her. Alex unleashed a shot and hit it in the back of the head. It turned and zoomed toward Alex as both he and Harmony kept firing at it.

"Foolish humans!" The demon created a vacuum and pulled the guns out of their hands. "You shall make a better vessel anyway," it said to Alex as it started becoming transparent. Acting quickly, I darted and grabbed its tail. It shrieked in shock as I spun it around in circles and hurled it toward the wall.

"No." I caught up and kicked it in the opposite direction. "One." I caught up again and thrashed it at the ceiling. "Threatens." I reached it and sent it plummeting to the floor. "My." I lifted him up and flung him at the wall again. "Friend!" I unleashed a barrage of exploding shurikens into him and watched him explode into nothingness.

"Daddy!" I turned and saw Harmony running to her dad. "Please hold on," she pleaded as she held him in her arms.

"I'm not down and out yet, honey," he coughed a few times and opened his eyes. His eyes opened up wide as she embraced him in a hug. "You were brilliant, sweetie. It's okay now."

"So, I hate to interrupt ya, but I gotta ask," I started, changing back to my human form. "What was that gas? You were shaking so badly." Alex glared at me, but I ignored him.

"It's basically holy water turned into refined gas." He laughed. "Now, you want to know the truth, right?" He motioned for Harmony to help him up to his feet. "If you really want to know how all of this, and yourself, came to be, you deserve it. Both of you, come here." Harmony helped him to the computer. I limped over and Alex followed. James pressed a few buttons, and a document popped up. "This is a log that I had kept from day one. It should answer every question you have, and some you didn't know you had." He rubbed Harmony's head. "Harmony and I will give you privacy. When you're done, we will be in the medic room next door." Alex stood beside me, and we watched them limped out of the room.

"You ready?" he asked once they were gone.

"I guess." I nodded. "I mean, as ready as I can be." I grabbed a chair and sat in front of the computer, scooting over to make room for Alex.

"All right then," he said, taking a seat and patting me on the back. "Let's get some answers."

Chapter Five

Log entry 172491: An interesting event had happened in the lab today. A shrouded figure, who called himself Loki, appeared to talk to me. He claims he is a demon who wants to give humanity a chance. He claims demons will soon be able to walk among us. He says their aim is to bring about the apocalypse early. I said I didn't believe him, and he said he would return with proof. Then, he vanished before my eyes. Perhaps I should have believed him.

Log Entry 172492: A boring day at the lab today. The new cancer drugs show no ill effect, which is good. I keep thinking about Loki. Is what he said true? If it is, why help us? I guess I need to wait for his return.

Log Entry 172493: Well today, Fred, the cancerous lab rat, died. RIP, Fred—your death proved that the cancer drug does have a very nasty side effect. Production of the drug has ceased until the cause is found. On a side note, I wonder when Loki is coming back.

Log Entry 172494: Loki came and visited today when I was getting ready for Fred's autopsy. He said that first, he would prove that demons can gather souls. Then he produced a white sphere out of thin air and placed it in Fred. And just like that, Fred was alive again. When he saw Loki, Fred bolted to the far corner of the room. Loki then produced a crystal ball that he called the "Orb of Vision." He had me touch it. What I saw had horrified me: numerous monstrosities in the middle of killing hundreds in single simple motions. I had jumped back after I saw one of them pointing right at me. I asked him why he would help us when he was obviously one of them. He said not to worry about his reasons and that, with his help, humanity would survive. I told him I would pull some strings and get grant money to start. He said he would return once I got the money before he vanished. I wonder how he will know when I get the grant money.

Log Entry 1724955: Well, since coming back to life, Fred has become a recluse. He refuses to leave the autopsy room. I guess returning to life must have been traumatic on the little guy.

Log Entry 1724956: Heard back from my contact in DC. We have a lunch date tomorrow, so I can explain everything to him. I told him I needed grant money but needed it to be classified. He said no, and then, I reminded him of the evidence I had destroyed for him. He said he would meet me tomorrow. Blackmail has its privileges.

"Blackmail in politics." Alex rolled his eyes. "I never would have imagined," he said, and I let out a chuckle. "Have you noticed that this guy writes like a child?" I smacked his stomach and stifled a laugh.

"Should we skip ahead?" I asked

"Up to you." He shrugged. "This may be the only time you get to see this though."

"Let's keep going then." I nodded, leaning back to get more comfortable.

> Log Entry 1724957: I had lunch with my contact today and told him why I needed the funding and secrecy. He didn't believe me, but after much arguing and me threatening to expose him, I got him to approve it. He said he would send it for "cancer research." I had to agree to show him what I had done in the way of advancement in a week. If there is no advancement or if I was lying to him, I would need to return the money. I sure hope Loki returns tomorrow.
>
> Log entry 1724958: Loki appeared today. He said he was impressed I was able to obtain the research money. He had a contract appear out of thin air and told me to sign it. I read it through and asked him why he wasn't taking my soul. I thought that was what all demons were after. He said human souls didn't interest him. He said that once I had signed it, I would have access to the knowledge and tools necessary for humanity to stand a chance, and in return, he would have access to me and my inventions. I took a deep, nervous breath and signed on the line. Immediately, the contract dissolved into a puff of black smoke. The smoke did a couple of circles before lunging into my shocked mouth. My head was instantly filled with visions of mythical creatures fighting back the demons and winning. I also saw weapons firing blasts of light instead of bullets and those lights creating holes in the demons they hit. When the visions ended, I noticed Loki smiling. I told him to return in

two days, and I would be ready to begin. Loki bowed and vanished.

Log Entry 1724959: Told my staff that we were ready for human testing on the new drug. There were objections, and those that objected were immediately fired. Many people lost their job today. Only two people remained—a nurse and a secretary. I told them to go home, and I would contact them when I was ready.

"So I'm guessing the two that stayed were our moms," Alex spoke up, which caused me to jump.

"That'd be my guess," I said, fidgeting.

"And that black smoke—" he started.

"Was probably the Possessor," I finished. "The only thing I don't get is why he had not named any names? Everyone is referred to in generic terms."

"Probably in case he was hacked or had to turn over his notes," Alex reasoned. "I mean, we already know he was dealing with illegal things"

"Good point." I nodded, turning back to the monitor.

Log entry 1724960: Loki had come by today. He produced numerous vials that were glowing in various colors. He told me they were souls of various mythical beasts and that he had gathered them during his interdimensional travels. He told me they held the key to fighting his brethren. He also produced a black vial and instructed me to coat my equipment with the substance. It would allow me to experiment on the soul, much like I would with any other liquid by binding it to the surface. He said he would let me get to work and return as needed. Then he vanished again.

Log Entry 1724961: Today, I have decided to only produce these logs as I make breakthroughs in my research. My Washington contact is coming soon, and I need something to show for it.

Log Entry 1724962: Well, this was an eventful day. My contact came to visit today and claimed I was lying and that the souls in the vials were only juices of various colors. Then, in spite of my objection, he proceeded to drink one of the vials. He dropped the vial and screamed out in pain, doubling over. He started to vomit blood before dropping dead. I began to panic because a dead Washington official would spell my end. That is when Loki appeared. He told me to calm down and that he would fix it. He waved his hand, and black smoke flew from his hand and into my contact. My contact then opened his eyes and knelt before Loki. Loki told him to return to his life and make sure I always had funding. My contact stood up, bowed, and left my lab. I asked Loki what had happened. Before vanishing, he said not to ask questions and continue my research.

"Wait, so does that mean there is a demon in the political game in DC?" asked Alex.

"That's how I read it, but I wouldn't worry about that," I replied.

"Why is that?"

"It's politics," I replied. "All politicians are demons to some degree. I'm sure he would fit right in." I smiled at him and continued reading.

Log Entry 1724963: After a few weeks of research, I determined the best way to place the souls of mythical beasts into humans is to inject it into a growing fetus. When I introduced some to human cells, the cells were instantly destroyed. The only time any cell survived was when I exposed the stem cells. If my hypothesis is correct, the stem cells should take in the foreign soul and act like a cocoon, protecting both the mother on the outside and the soul itself. Now, I've just got to convince my test subject and the nurse to let me test this out.

Log Entry 1724964: I feel like I won the lottery today. Just by chance, both my nurse and secretary became pregnant. After much convincing and pleading, I got the secretary to agree. I had to promise that her family would always be taken care of. My nurse made me promise the same thing for her in exchange for her silence while she assisted me. I agreed without thinking. After all, it's not my money, and the world must be saved.

Log Entry 1724965: The test subject's lab results came back, and today, Project Cocoon began. Using ultrasound technology, I injected dragon soul into the growing fetus. Almost immediately, her heart rate spiked up, and she developed a fever. I began to worry that the soul might escape the fetus through the umbilical cord. However, after two hours, her vitals returned to normal. I have determined that the substance Loki gave me to bind the soul must be harmful to humans. No more human subjects until I can remedy this.

Log Entry 1724966: I believe I have managed to duplicate the chemical makeup of one of the souls. It shows no sign of life; maybe it'll work in weapon form. I only have a limited number of souls, and this, I could mass produce. Further study is needed.

Log Entry 1724967: I was visited by an angel today. They told me what I was doing is forbidden and all research must stop. They said that I must leave humanity's fate up to Him. The angel then proceeded to destroy all the vials that I had sitting out. He warned me to stop all research before he vanished.

Log Entry 1724968: Had an ultrasound done to check on the baby. It has survived past the first trimester. It seems the nurse and the sub-ject have become close to one another. They talk about weekend plans all the time. Loki showed up, and I told him what had happened. He said not to worry and just to care for the child. He sensed two souls in it and knew that I had suc-ceeded. After it's born, he will help me keep experimenting undetected. It's important to keep the baby unknown for now though.

Log Entry 1724969: I found out that both the subject and the nurse are having boys today. They told me they would raise them together. The subject said that they figure it'd be nice for the boys to always have a friend. She said it was also nice her friend was a nurse because we don't know how the kid will turn out since he will grow up with two souls.

Log Entry 1724970: Well, the subject's baby was born today. We delivered him in the daycare wing on the top floor. So far, Project Cocoon is going well. I allowed a commemorative picture to celebrate two healthy baby boys introduced to the world. Except for a dark mark on his hand, the subject appears completely normal. For their safety, I hope no angels or demons find out.

Log Entry 1724971: Loki came to visit today. I expressed concern that the subject appears completely human. He told me not to worry. He still sensed two souls within him. He said he would return with a way for me to work in secret once the child goes home.

Log Entry 1724972: Everyone left today. I instructed the nurse to call me periodically with updates. I assured them they would both continue to receive deposits at the first of the month. Now, I just need to wait for Loki to return.

Log Entry 1724973: Loki has created an underground lab for me and replenished my stock of souls after the angel had destroyed them. He said that the lab uses his demonic powers to camouflage us and keep us hidden, and that should be from both angels and demons. It seems to be true; I've been working for two years without interruption. I had managed to create a few safety measures too, once I managed to decipher the camouflage shield.

Log Entry 1724974: There was an attack today. Demons had managed to conjure a portal inside the burger joint across the street. They attacked fast; there were no survivors. I used this opportunity to test my defenses. I launched a micro bomb into the portal. There was a chain reaction, and the building imploded on itself as the portal closed. I learned that, while it works, I must only use it in areas without civilians.

Log Entry 1724975: I gave the boy a checkup today before school starts, so I could sign on the required paperwork as his primary care doctor. The mother pulled me aside with concerns about sending him to school, knowing what's inside of him. She said, when his temper flairs, his strength grows to epic proportions. I assured her that he appears completely human, but until he learns to control his temper, it might be better to give him mood suppressors to keep him calm.

"Well, that explains why I was medicated through most of elementary school," I said, tapping my finger in frustration a few times against the desk. Alex just nodded.

Log Entry 1724976: The test subject notified me she was pregnant again. I decided against injecting the fetus with anything. I am yet to find out the cause of the allergic reaction from last time. I also cannot be certain if the entire soul is in the first child or if there is residues left in the subject. I also cannot risk alerting the angels that I still am working in spite of the threat I was given.

Log Entry 1724977: The test subject had a baby girl. She had her delivery here again. Loki came to visit while I was monitoring the baby in the nursery. He told me that the baby only had one human soul. He asked why I hadn't injected this child. I told him that I wasn't putting this family in anymore danger than I already have. He got angry and said I shouldn't put all my efforts on one child even if he has a royal dragon soul within him. He disappeared, and I stared at the baby wondering if I had made the right choice.

"So that dragon in you is a member of royalty?" Alex asked. "I assume you'll want me to start calling you 'Your Majesty.'"

"It does have a nice ring to it." I nodded, dodging his hand as he smacked the back of my head. *How come you didn't tell me?*

Memories of that life are just that, he responded. *What I was doesn't matter. All that matters is the now. Right now, you and I are intrinsically linked. I've become the shadow to your light, the yin to your yang.*

I'm sorry. I felt horrible.

Don't be. You didn't steal my soul. You didn't choose to inject it into yourself. You're a victim too, he chastised. It was strangely comforting.

I swear to you, I will figure out a way to help you. I meant it.

> Log Entry 1724978: Tragedy struck today. I had a spike on my radar over the subject's home, and I sent a drone to investigate. I spotted both the subject and the nurse's families lying lifeless. I could not spot the child though. Hopefully, he is still alive and well. I will have to ask my daughter if she knows the boys and if they will be in school tomorrow. I torched the house and called in a few favors to hide the true cause of death.

"He set the fire!" I exclaimed, standing up and stepping away from the computer. I kept pacing, trying to wrap my head around what I had just read. "He set the house on fire."

"Breathe, dude." Alex grabbed me to stop me from pacing.

"How am I supposed to breathe?" I snapped. "Our families didn't die in a fire. They were murdered."

"Yeah, but not by him," Alex reassured. "Not by human hands."

"I know, but he hid the truth!" I shouted, pointing to the door they had gone through.

"What was he supposed to do, Sam?" Alex snapped. "Tell the world that our parents were killed by demons because of experiments? No one would believe him."

The truth suddenly hit me like a ton of rocks. "It's my fault," I mumbled, slumping over.

"What do you mean?"

"If something supernatural killed our families, it's my fault," I spilled out, not being able to look at him. "I'm sorry."

"It's not your fault." I tensed away when he came up to put his arm around me.

"Yes, it is," I said as I curled up in the chair. "Whatever killed them was after me—not you, not them. I had pushed really, really hard to get them to let us go on that trip. If I was there, they—"

"Would still be dead." Alex finished.

"But—"

"No buts." Alex sat down next to me and placed his hand on my knee. I tensed a little and continued to look down. "Look at me," he said. I sighed before looking up and into his gentle eyes. "You didn't do anything wrong. If we were home, we would both be dead or worse. The creatures that did that wanted you dead, just like they do now. There would be no negotiating or trading with them. You can't blame yourself, man." He held me in a hug. "You're a victim too." I sat there for a few minutes and let myself cry. Alex let me cry and didn't move until I was done.

I promise you this, vessel. Just like you swear to find a way to help me, I swear to help you. Tiamat tried to comfort me. *We will find those responsible for your families' deaths, and we will crush them.* At that, I actually laughed, which caused Alex to let go.

"Thank you," I said, while wiping away the last of the tears. "Both of you." Alex looked confused for a second, and I tapped my birthmark. He nodded, understanding at once.

"You okay now?" he asked.

"I'm better." I nodded. "The hero of this story can't be a quivering mess, can he?" I laughed, trying to sound confident. "Look." I pointed to the screen. "We are almost at the end of the document. Let's finish this and see about going home." Alex nodded and turned back to the screen.

> Log entry 172979: Spoke to my daughter, and she asked around. She found out that both boys were on a school trip. While I am happy that the boy still lives, and with him the world's hope, I realize he is still orphaned. I will make

sure he and the nurse's child are both taken care of. I will reveal the truth when the time is right.

Log Entry 1724980: Demons attacked a senior party at the park today. The child was there, and he accepted his destiny today. Loki said that he single-handedly pushed them back, and only one child lost his soul in the process. Loki said he spoke to the child after he somehow managed to reign the dragon back in and began telling him the truth. He had to leave when the police showed up. The cops, Loki said, took them in for questioning, but he would watch over him and guide him here.

Log Entry 1724981: Loki came today and told me that the dragon is dead. I asked him what had happened. He told me that a dragon-slaying demon was sent to the station to kill him. He tried to get him to leave, but he refused to leave his friend behind. He had him take his friend and said he would fight the demon. Loki told me to find another solution to fight the demons and the chance of the dragon winning was zero. Then, he vanished in an angry huff. I can't believe all my work is down the tubes. I need to find another solution, and fast.

"Think Loki still thinks you're dead?" Alex asked as I shut down the computer.

"Oh, I wouldn't say that." Alex and I spun around at the voice to see Loki standing on the opposite side of the room. "I must say I'm surprised though. How did you manage to survive Asura's assault?"

"Let's just say that Tiamat and I make a great team," I returned as Alex and I stood up. I instinctively stood between Loki and Alex.

"Relax, boy," Loki chortled. "If I had wanted your friend dead, I would have done it when you were fighting Asura." He began to circle around me. "I never would have imagined the dragon crystal shard I gave you had that much power." I tensed as he mentioned the crystal. "That's right. you can't hide the truth from me. I know it gave you power, but I just don't know how." He stopped and stared right at me with his arms crossed. "Let's play a game," he suggested.

"Depends on the game," I answered.

"Let's take turns asking each other questions." He sat down where Alex and I had been sitting. "I answer one question, then you answer one question honestly."

"Fair enough. First question: which demon had killed our families?" I asked before Alex could object.

"I haven't heard anyone claim it, but it wasn't necessarily a demon," he answered.

"What does that mean?" I asked

"Now, now, I answered your question. My turn first," he chided. "How did the crystal give you the power to defeat Asura?"

"It allowed Tiamat and I to fuse," I answered.

"Fascinating, and how does that work?" He got wide-eyed, almost like a child being given candy.

"One question at a time, remember?" I threw back, wiping the smile on his face away. "So what do you mean by not necessarily a demon?"

"It's simple," he answered. "Several demons are fallen angels, and in order to make sure the professor's sensors work, I had to make it detect angels too." I bit my tongue and waited for his question. "How does this fusion work?" he asked.

"I don't fully understand it myself," I began. "From what I can tell, the crystal acts like a medium. Tiamat puts his soul in it, and I can channel Tiamat through it," I tried to explain. "So are you saying angels killed our families?"

"I'm not accusing anyone from either side," he declared, holding up his hands in defense. "I'm just telling you it's a possibility. I haven't heard anyone talking in the underworld, and angels aren't always, well, angels." He smiled at me, and chills ran down my spine. "Final question: How did you find this place on your own?"

"Family photo albums that weren't destroyed," I answered. "And knowledge of town history."

"Humans were always resourceful," he chuckled. "Since you played my little game, let me give you an advice. Before I bested my prior master, he mentioned a blade that is capable of slaying both angels and demon alike. I suggest you find it."

"Where is it?"

"Dunno." He shrugged. "Don't even have a name, but I know it exists at least. My master never lied. He was just too proud." He stood up. "You're resourceful. I'm sure, between you and the professor, you will find it." He bowed. "Until next time, dragon." And with that, he was gone.

"You okay, man?" Alex asked, his hand on my shoulder.

"I'm not sure," I answered. "I mean, I knew we'd probably find some things out about our parents that we probably wouldn't want to. I'm fine with that stuff. At least, I think so. But to think they were killed by angels who are supposed to be kind and just. Does that mean I'm evil? Am I that big of an abomination that angels would want me dead? If I am, does that mean I have no chance to see them again? Am I now destined for eternal purgatory?" I began to hyperventilate.

"Let's take things one step at a time, Sam," Alex reasoned with me. "We don't know they were killed by angels. He just said it was possible." He grabbed my shoulder again. "And you aren't evil. Evil wouldn't have saved Harmony, let alone Megan. I know you don't like her."

"That was because you were there," I interjected. "If you weren't there, I couldn't have regained control."

"Exactly! *You* regained control," he said, thumping my chest. "*You* stopped from hurting Megan. *You* saved Harmony. Everything *you* do is good. The two souls in you just clashed originally. Things have worked themselves out, and you *are* good. I bet my life on it." He smiled, and I followed suit. "Better?" he asked.

I kept smiling. "Yeah, thanks again."

"Anytime," he laughed and threw his arm over me. "Someone has to keep you in line." He dodged my elbow jab and pulled me to the door the professor had passed through. "Now, let's go find the professor and decide on our next move."

Chapter Six

"We need to find the blade of legend that can slay both angels and demons," I reiterated as we, Alex and I, walked into the medic bay of the lab.

"Does this mean you are still going to help us and accept your destiny?" the professor asked as he sat up and removed the monitors from his chest. Harmony shot me a deathly glare which Alex must have noticed.

"How's the professor, Harmony?" Alex asked, trying to cool her down by changing the subject.

"His vitals are improving, but they are still weak," she answered.

"They are improving though," he answered. "Which means we can get back to the subject we are all here for." He turned to his daughter. "Saving the world."

"I guess," she conceded. "As long as you *promise* me to take it easy and not overdo it," she added. He held up his arms in defense. "I promise," he said before turning back to me. "So are you going to help us then?"

"I still don't know," I admitted. "I know that, either way, I want to find that blade." I looked at Alex and then back at the professor. "The only thing I know for sure is that I want to protect those dear to me. If that means stopping the apocalypse, then so be it. For the time being, our goals are the same."

"Fair enough," he submitted. He walked over to a computer and logged in. "So does this blade have a name?"

"I'm sure it does, but I don't know what it is."

"How do you know it even exists then?" Harmony retorted.

"Because Loki told us it did," Alex answered. Harmony and the professor both stopped what they were doing and turned to look at us. "Did I just say something funny?"

"Loki was here?" Harmony asked, rapidly pressing buttons on her computer. "The alarm wasn't triggered this time." She pressed a few more button. "It still shows it's active though."

"Did he build himself an immunity, or is something wrong with it?" the professor asked out loud. Then he struck his fist down on the table. "Damn!"

"Someone want to fill us in?" I asked.

"The demon sensor I built," he stated. "Whenever Loki appeared in the past, it always went off. This time, he was as far as *in* our lab, and nothing was tripped."

"My guess would be he found a way to be immune to it. I mean, he helped you build it, right? He would know about its weaknesses," I reasoned. "I mean, is it possible he froze time when he walked in here? If it was frozen, the alarms wouldn't even know he was here."

"That sounds possible." Harmony nodded, trying to reassure her father.

"I agree, but I just don't like not knowing if we are sitting ducks to an attack." He closed his eyes and took a deep breath. Then turned to me, he said, "So what all did Loki tell you?"

"All he said was his master had never lied and that he had told him about the blade. He never told him its name or where it was hidden, just that it existed."

"Of course, that was helpful." Harmony rolled her eyes. All of a sudden, I jumped as a siren went off.

"What's that?" I shouted as I covered my ears.

"The alarm we were wondering about," Harmony shouted as she and her father ran out the door. "Follow us!" she ordered, popping her head back in. Alex and I looked at each other before taking off behind her. We ran down the halls and through a door. The room was lined with monitors from wall to wall. Harmony and her dad stood on opposite ends and observed the keys below them.

"It's in town somewhere." James pushed a flashing button, and the alarm shut off.

"Bringing it up on all the monitors now." Harmony flipped a switch, and all the monitors switched to the same thing. We saw a female demon with wings walking calmly through town, heading toward a lone building.

"What's that building?" Alex asked.

"That would be the..." Harmony keyed in a few things, and the visuals zoomed in. We all grew pale. "The city day care."

"I'm on it," I declared.

"But there are guards with guns there. And those guards want to hurt you," Alex reminded me. "Besides, how are you going to get there in time? It's across the city."

"I have to do something to earn their trust, don't I?" I blurted out. "Besides, these are innocent toddlers who have done nothing wrong. I've got to do something." Alex started to object. "Look, I'll be fine. I promise," I said, pulling him in for a hug. "I'll be back soon. Stay here and help these guys research the blade. That's my next objective." I stepped back and transformed into the ninja.

"I respect your morals, but that doesn't explain how you are going to get there in time to save the kids," Harmony said.

Teleport, Tiamat suggested.

What? I asked.

The crystal used to allow teleportation. That's how we got around our planet so fast. You should be able to access it as well.

Sounds like a plan, but how do I teleport exactly?

That's up to you. I didn't have the crystal inside me at the time. We had a device to access it.

Right. Well, here goes nothing then. I closed my eyes and focused on the crystal.

"Hello, are you even listening to me?" Harmony asked, annoyed.

"Honestly, probably not." Alex laughed. "He gets like that when he's talking to the dragon inside him. There's no real way to get through to him until he finishes talking to him."

"I think I've got my mode of transport. Keep each other safe, you guys. I'll be back before too long. Find some info on the blade please." I stepped out the room to make distance, not knowing what would happen. "And I heard that, Alex." I closed my eyes and focused on the crystal, and I felt it flowing through me when I opened my eyes. "Ninja, teleport!" I assumed a ninjutsu pose and felt myself flying swiftly. I pictured the inside of the day care, and I felt drawn to it. All of a sudden, the movement stopped, and I was there, standing inside the day care. The winged demon appeared startled as I appeared inches from it. It shrieked and kicked me back. I flew through the air and crashed against the wall. I stood up, shaking. I looked around and saw motionless soldiers in front of the door. Children were being shielded by the workers, and one lone soldier stood pointing his gun at me.

"Don't move!" he shouted, his gun shaking as he pointed at me. "I will shoot."

"Look, I know you don't trust me. I know that your bosses say I'm evil, but I'm not." I held up my hands. "Let me kill this thing and protect the children. Then I will leave."

"But..." I could see the hesitation in his eyes.

"Look, this thing killed your comrades, and your guns did nothing, right?" I quickly reasoned as the demon made its way through the wall I had crashed through. "I don't have time to argue. I promise I won't hurt you all. If I come back in after I finish this thing, then blast away. Okay?" I ran toward it and launched myself, sending it back with me. I built up enough speed and sent us flying through the glass doors. "You're not getting to the kids, you...whatever you are."

"That would be a harpy," she smirked before clawing at my shoulder. I shrieked, letting go. "And you would be the famed dragon."

"And you would be sentient, it seems." I stood up and gripped my shoulder. "So give up now, and I'll let you live." I smirked.

"I can't do that," she said, flapping her wings to hover in the air. "Children souls are powerful. They go a long way in opening the door for our master," she cackled. "I can take great pleasure in killing you though. You slew Asura, the one demon that I considered a friend." She flew at me with incredible speed. "Now DIE!"

"Not gonna happen," I said, leaping above and coming down with great speed. I hit her back and sent her crashing into the ground. She stood up and tried to take off again before crying in pain as she looked at her wing. When she had crash-landed, it had broken.

"I'll just tear you apart on the ground then," she said, running at me. I simply side-stepped and roundhoused. She went flying into the side of the building across the street. I jumped over to her in a single leap as she struggled to turn and face me.

"I almost feel guilty," I admitted. "I will make your death quick. I'm sorry you couldn't get your revenge." I gathered an energy shuriken and placed it on her neck. "Goodbye," I bid before walking away. Without looking back, I snapped my fingers. She let out a quick cry, and there was a small explosion. I turned back around in time to see her body turn to dust and blow away.

"Is it gone?" came a question. I turned around to notice a little boy come running out.

"It is." I nodded in affirmation.

"That was so *cool*!" he exclaimed as he ran up to me. I jumped back so he wouldn't touch me and burn. "I'm not afraid of you. I saw you save us," he said, starting a walk toward me again. We both turned when we heard a gun cock. The surviving soldier was staring at me; his gun aimed at my head.

"He came running to me. I can't control the actions of others," I defended.

"I know, and that's the only reason you are still standing," he replied coldly. "Now leave!"

The little boy raised his arms, as if blocking my body with his. "You can't hurt him...I won't let you! He's not a bad guy." He stood bravely.

"Andrew, get back here this instant!" The day care worker stepped outside and yelled out.

"But...," he wavered before standing up straight again.

"It's okay, Andrew," I said as he turned to face me. "The soldier is just doing his job protecting you, much like my job is to fight the bad guys." I crouched down to eye level. "Don't be mad at him for doing his job. He was told by his bosses, who got some bad information that I'm a bad guy too."

"I'll make sure to spread the word that you're good. I'm the most popular here," he boasted and smiled. I couldn't help but smile too.

"Andrew, get in here, now!" The worker tried again.

"Go on back before you get in trouble." I ushered him as I stood up. "I'm leaving anyway." I waved at the officer before teleporting back to the lab.

"Excellent job!" The professor raved when I reappeared. "I was right about you." I undid my transformation and let him talk for a while, spacing out and not listening.

They do think I'm the enemy, I moped to Tiamat. *That soldier's eyes were so determined to see me dead.*

I don't think he wanted to see you completely dead. He never shot at you, Tiamat answered. *I think you will be able to reach out to humanity eventually. You won't always be the villain. The child seemed to take to you quickly.*

The innocence of youth. I smirked. *He was standing up to that armed guard without thinking.*

Hope that humanity will win, he murmured.

"So I think the next step..." I snapped out of the conversation as the professor excitedly kept talking about the next step in the war.

"I'm sorry, but I think I'm done for the day," I shot out.

"Oh, okay," he replied, sounding dejected.

"Look, I'm just tired. I've been through a lot today, and I just want to find Alex and go home." I tried to sound sympathetic.

"I understand. He's in the library with Harmony researching this mystery blade." He pointed down the hall. "Third door on the right. Harmony will walk you out." I started to walk that way. "Oh, before you go, I want to give you something. Follow me." He walked toward the room we had read the logs in. I sighed and followed him. He went to where Harmony retrieved the guns from and grabbed one that was left in there. Then he walked to the computer desk and pulled out two watch-like devices. He handed me one of them.

"What is it?" I asked.

"This will let me track and communicate with you at all times. If you need to talk to me, press the button at the bottom and hold it when you talk. It's like a walkie-talkie." He pointed at the button as I put it on. "I have a second one for Alex as well as a gun he could use to defend himself in an emergency." He handed them to me. "The gun tends to overheat if used rapidly. It's still a prototype, but as you know, it does its job in a pinch. I will try to keep perfecting it tonight. Now, go get some rest." He walked and sat down at the computer. I watched for a minute before walking out the door to the library.

"Do you think this might be a clue?" Alex asked, pointing at a spot in a book he was holding as I walked into the library.

"No. That can't be it," Harmony replied, shaking her head. "That's a holy blade. There is no way it would slay angels too."

"Can we go home now?" I asked, causing Alex to jump in surprise. He smiled when he noticed me.

"You're back," he exclaimed and came running to hug me. I just stood in one place. He noticed my stiffness. "You okay, man?"

"I will be, just tired," I responded, faking a yawn. "Can we just go home now?"

"Yeah, that's probably a good idea." He kept his arm over my shoulder. "I feel like Harmony and I are just going around in circles with our research anyway."

"Well, *some* of us are going circles," she shot out, and Alex flipped her off. They laughed, and I couldn't help but join in. "Come on," she said, setting her book down. "I'll show you guys out. Not all of us can teleport where we want to." This time, I flipped her off, and we all laughed again. The walk out of the building was quiet, but not tense like our walk in. When we reached the car, I threw Alex my keys. He nodded and slid into the driver's seat.

"I will talk to you tomorrow at school about my findings," Harmony said as Alex started the car.

"I don't know if I'm going to be going anymore," I answered.

"It'll be fine. Alex told me you were worried about what Megan had told her dad. Even if everyone at school knows, you will still have two friends there, and the army wouldn't dare attack you in human form. The press would have a field day with that, and the panic would be astronomic," she tried to reason with me. "If you don't try to have a normal life, she will probably send her daddy's men to your house to 'rescue' Alex." A pen came flying from behind me and hit Harmony in the face.

"Don't listen to her, man, let's just talk at home," Alex promptly spoke up. I nodded and got in the car.

"I'm sorry, I was just…," Harmony began

"It's okay. I told you some subjects are a little touchy." Alex said. "At the very least, we will talk to you tomorrow somehow." He drove off, and I watched Harmony in the mirror looking at us as we drove away.

"I'm beat." I let out a sigh and reclined my seat.

"Yeah, but that's not the only reason you wanted out. I know that yawn in there wasn't real," he said, glancing at me.

"It is, and it isn't," I answered, resting my arm over my eyes. "It was emotionally tiring as well as physically. Every adult at the day care saw me as their enemy. The only one that stood up for me was a young kid."

"Not everyone saw you as evil, man. That's a good sign," he offered.

"I know…I sighed, but it still sucks to be looked at as the villain. I don't think I can face our whole school that way, man."

"Then, we won't. We will not go to school again. It's that simple." He declared.

"No, it's not. I want you to go, man." I pleaded.

He stood his ground. "Not without you."

"Yes, without me. Harmony will be there and will probably have information on the blade. She seems like the type who won't sleep until she has, at least, some clue. She's right about Megan too," I sighed.

"I don't think…," he began.

"No, you know she's right. If you don't show up at school in a day or two, she will send out a search party. I don't worry about you being at school without me either since the professor gave me these." I pulled out the other watch and gun. "We can stay in communication—without cell service even—with this. And this is another one of those guns you had used against the demon before. We know it will, at least, slow them down until I get there."

"But…" he started to say.

"Look, just go until we find the blade," I said. "I promise I won't do anything reckless without telling you first. Once we get a clue on the blade, you can come with me."

"Says the one who was going to ditch me this morning," he pouted.

"Fair enough," I admitted, and silence enveloped the rest of the trip home. We walked into the house and locked the doors behind us, and I broke the silence. "Look, I'm sorry. I know I'm being selfish asking you to go without me."

"Yes, you are," he replied coldly.

"It's just that I'm scared." I hung my head.

"About demons attacking while you're there? Those attacking the day care proves otherwise!" He raised his voice. "About Megan getting the army to shoot you? I don't think she has that much power. About you being an outsider? Sorry to burst your bubble, but you kind of were before all this."

"Yes, to all of the above!" I shouted back. "But none of those are the main reason."

"What is it then?" he shouted, frustrated to the maximum.

"It's *you*! Okay?" I quivered, and he stood still in shock.

"How is it me?" his voice calmed down. "I thought I'd handled everything well. I told you, I don't care what happens. I'm in this until the end with you."

"Exactly," I agreed. "The problem isn't the way you are. I don't want to hurt you." He started to speak, but I kept going. "I don't mean physically. I've got full faith in my other half. I mean emotionally. I know I've always been the outsider, especially since our families were killed. I know you've always defended me, even when I didn't hear it. This time though, I'm considered public enemy number one. I know that if I go, Megan will make you choose. I don't want to make you choose. I don't want to make everyone hate you too."

"Dude, there's no choice to make." He brought me in for a hug. After that, he held my arms and got in my face, so I *had* to look at him. "There's no choice. It's always been, and always will be, you and me. If she tries to make you enemy number one, if she propagates an attack on you at all, I will warn her of this tonight." He pulled out his phone and sent a message. "If she hurts you at all tomorrow, she and I are finished."

"But…" I struggled with words, unsure of what to say. "I'm sorry."

"No, I'm sorry. I never meant to make you think I'd ever choose her over our friendship. If that means I would become the most unpopular and hated jock at school, then so be it." He hugged me again and laughed. "I've got big shoulders. I can take it." He flexed a little while pointing to his shoulders, and I couldn't help but laugh. "So does that mean you're coming to school with me tomorrow?" he asked, giving me a cheesy grin.

"All right," I sighed, rolling my eyes and throwing my hands up in defeat. "You win. I will try and return to school tomorrow with you."

"Then let's rest up." He went into the kitchen to heat up some dinner. "Tomorrow is going to be yet another big day in our lives!" he shouted through the walls.

Chapter Seven

"What is *he* doing here?" Megan seethed as I followed Alex into our first period.

"He is going to class, just like the rest of us." Alex took his seat next to her and motioned for me to sit on the other side. Harmony came in and sat beside me.

"But he—" she began to shout, and Alex hushed her up.

"He saved us," Alex retorted in a hushed whisper. "And he is still a student of this school." He sat back and crossed his arms. "Besides, you shouldn't be surprised. I texted you what the deal was last night, and you said you understood."

"Doesn't mean the freak would actually show up," she huffed. "The freak has bailed on plans before." I slouched back in my seat.

"Don't let her get to you," Harmony whispered in my ear. I could feel her rubbing my back.

"Look, the freak can't even handle this attention," she cackled. I felt the other students ogling at me. Alex noticed this too and slammed his hands down on his desk.

"That's it!" He stood up and looked down at her. "We are done!"

"Surely you're ki-kidding," she stammered. "We are the power couple of this school. You can't dump me...especially not over him."

"I think I did." He sat down again, his chest puffed out.

"I can't believe this!" Megan grabbed her stuff and stormed out, stopping at the door only to point at me and add, "This isn't over. No one beats me." I sat stunned at what had just happened. I was trying to figure out what she meant by that when Alex stood back up and faced the class.

"Let me just say one thing," he began, "Sam here is my best friend. If I see or hear any of you giving him trouble, you will have to go through me. Is that clear?" The silence in the room was deafening as he paused for a response. "Thought so," he finished. As he sat down, I couldn't help but smile. The rest of first period went by without a hitch.

"I wonder where Megan went. She never came back to class," Harmony mused as we walked past the halls to our next class.

"Probably up to no good," I answered.

"I still don't think she would do anything drastic," Alex said with doubt in his voice.

"She is probably still crying in the girl's locker room about how you had the nerve to dump her," Harmony mocked, throwing her hand on her forehead in mock anguish.

"You're enjoying this, aren't you?" Alex asked. She nodded vigorously.

I noticed Megan standing outside the next classroom, a wicked smile plastered on her face. I stopped in my tracks. "I'm still going to go with she's up to no good."

"Why do you say that?" Alex asked.

"Cause her smile right now is creeping me out," I said, pointing at her. She waved and pointed me to the guard standing in front of the classroom.

"I'm not gonna leave your side, dude." Alex said, realizing Megan had betrayed his faith.

"Me neither," Harmony added.

"Oh my god," I muttered when I recognized the guard.

"What is it?" Alex asked.

"That's the same guard who was guarding the day care," I answered, the color draining from my face.

"The one who wouldn't listen to you?" Harmony asked.

"It's not that he didn't listen to me. If that was the case, I'd be dead. It's that he follows all his orders to a T."

"So what do we do?" Alex asked. "Run?"

"No, that would just look worse," I said. "I think I just gotta talk to him and see where this leads." I turned to nod at Harmony and then at Alex. I took a deep breath and walked to the guard.

"Right behind ya, man." Alex encouraged as he and Harmony followed close behind me.

"So we meet again," the officer said with a slight smile. "I've got orders to take you into custody."

"For what? He's done nothing wrong!" Harmony belted out.

"He's a monster who destroys all in his path," he replied.

"Like the day care?" Alex asked.

"He would have if I wasn't there," he said with pride.

"It's fine guys, I'll go," I said, raising my hand before they could argue with the guard. He cuffed my hands and marched me down the halls of our school, his gun pointed at my back. Alex and Harmony followed close behind.

"You guys aren't wanted. You are free to go," he said to them as he walked.

"Then we are free to follow," Harmony responded.

"Yup, I promised I'd stay with him, and I will keep that promise," Alex said, and I smiled.

"Fine, whatever," he sneered.

"So, how's Andrew?" I asked as we approached the army tents stationed outside the school.

"Andrew?" he questioned, flashing his badge to the officer guarding the entrance to the mobile base.

"The kid from the day care who came out to watch. You know, the little troublemaker." I smiled, remembering him trying to hug me.

"Every civilian from the day care is alive and well," he responded, opening the door to a makeshift cell and pushed me in. Alex and Harmony quickly slipped in before he could shut the door. He sighed when he noticed them in there.

"That's good," I smiled in genuine relief. I noticed a fleeting look of shock on his face before changing back to stern again.

"The general will be here to question you soon," he said before walking off.

"I don't get it. Why did you turn yourself in?" Harmony asked. I started to answer, but Alex took over; he already knew why.

"He didn't want to start a fight in the school. If he winds up fighting the military, he didn't want it to be in school where innocent people could get hurt," he explained, and I nodded. "He is sick of being considered the villain, and he's doing everything he can to change that. His enemy isn't humanity, it's demons."

"I know that," Harmony sighed, sitting back in the far corner. "It's just…couldn't we have run?"

"That would have made things look even worse," I answered. "If we ran away, I would appear to be the villain they perceive me to be. Who knows what they would have said about you two as well. I can't stand the thought of anything happening to Alex, and you are slowly growing on me as well." Harmony stuck her tongue out at that statement.

"Gee, thanks," she threw out, and we all broke into a laugh.

"How long do you think he's going to make us wait?" Alex asked, and as if on cue, the door swung open.

"I don't keep my guests waiting very long," announced an older man, walking into the tent escorted by the same guard. "I am General Kalvin Lee Cooshings. I lead the group of men sent here to protect the city." I observed the general up close. His face was worn, and it showed the horrors it had faced. Even at his age, he looked like he could hold his own in combat if the need arose. "The man behind me, you have already met. This is Officer Jason Wyatt Mathers. He insisted he be the one to bring you in."

"It's a pleasure, sir," I said, standing up straight, hands still cuffed in front. "Can I ask how you knew I was the dragon everyone is looking for?"

"The mayor called, and he told us he had heard from a source that you were the one we've been hunting," he replied, and Alex's shoulders slumped forward in depression. "So I take it that the source was correct. You are the dragon, then?"

"Yes, it's true," I said, looking him straight in the eyes, and didn't falter. "I am the dragon. I—"

"Shall I shoot him then, sir?" Jason pulled out his gun and aimed it straight at me. "He has confirmed your suspicion after all." Alex got up and came to stand between us.

"Stand down, Mathers," General Cooshings ordered. Jason wavered, putting the gun down. Alex took a breath of relief. "Something still bothers me. If you are the dragon, why didn't you fight your capture? If Officer Mathers's report about the attack is correct, you could have easily escaped."

"It is because I took a chance," I started. "I wanted to meet you and explain this myself: I am not evil. My goal is to stop the demons. Save humanity, not destroy it. The mayor's source is vain and petty, and she had determined that because I started to attack her, before I could control myself, that I must be evil. Even if that's not the case, the fact that I've always been a thorn in her side is reason enough for her to lie to you."

"How do we know you are not lying to us now?" he asked.

"I don't think he is, sir," Jason spoke up. Alex, Harmony, and I looked at each other in shock.

"I don't think he is either, Mathers," he admitted. "I just want to see if he can prove it."

"I can't prove that I'm not lying," I stated. "I can prove that I *am* the dragon and that, if I wanted to, I could break the three of us out of here in a moment. I can prove that these handcuffs"—I held my arms up—"could have been broken the second he put them on. Will that help my case?"

"It might," he admitted. "Either way, please go ahead. I would like to see the dragon for myself." I nodded and went to the center of the room. Alex ushered for them to stand back, and they did. I transformed, and both the general and officer went wide-eyed. I used an energy shuriken to slice through the handcuffs as though they were made of butter. I brought my arms to my side and stood before the general. "Marvelous!" he cried out in excitement. Suddenly, another guard burst into the room.

"Sorry to interrupt your interrogation, sir, but we have an emergency!" He was out of breath and gasping for air, as though he had run around the whole base looking for the general.

"Well, spit it out then," Cooshings urged. The officer stared at my other form and stayed silent. Cooshings followed his gaze and saw he was afraid to speak. "Do not fear this dragon, officer. Not only have we captured him"—he stared at me for a reaction; I didn't give one—"We have managed to reach a treaty with him. He is on our side now, and we will *win* because of him."

No longer the enemy, Tiamat said to me. *You are right. There is hope for humanity yet.* I smiled and turned to see my friends smiling too.

"Are you sure?" the officer asked.

"You dare question your general?" Mathers barked. "Now, what is this emergency you panicked in about?"

"My apologies, sir," he saluted promptly and continued about the emergency. "An unknown demon has launched an assault on the city hospital," he said. "The team guarding it has almost been wiped out."

"And the civilians?" Cooshings asked.

"The hospital began moving patients to the bomb shelter when the attack began. It is not known how many are left to move and how many can even be moved."

"All right. Have our remaining forces—" the general began.

"General, if I may?" I interrupted him. I saw his temper flare for a moment, but then he nodded for me to continue. "Have your troops retreat within the hospital walls. I'll handle the demon." I turned to my companions. "You two head to the lab and grab the weapons that are ready and bring them back."

"But—" Harmony started to say.

"There's no time to argue. People, sick people, are at risk right now. Besides"—I turned to face the general and Mathers—"I think we have reached an agreement that I am not the current enemy, right?"

"That's right," Cooshings nodded. "Officer, do as he says. Tell them the dragon is on his way, and he is not the enemy. They are *not* to open fire at him."

"Yes, sir," he saluted and ran off to relay the message.

"I still have questions for you," Cooshings barked at me. "You need to come back when you're done."

"Fair enough." I nodded. "Alex, stay safe getting the weapons."

"Right back at ya," he said, giving me a thumbs-up. "See you after you trash that thing." He and Harmony took off for the lab.

"Be back soon." I bid adieu to Cooshings and Mathers and teleported to the hospital.

I appeared behind the demon as he prepared to crush the soldier in front of him. I patted his shoulder and dodged as he swung his arm around. I waved my finger at him, chiding, "Don't you know it's impolite to pick on people smaller than you?" I attempted to roundhouse him when he caught my foot and tossed me crashing into the wall. I rolled out of the way when a part of the roof dropped down from the impact.

"If it isn't the dragon," its voice boomed. I stood up and got a better look at my foe. He was big and bulky and appeared to be made of stone. "The bounty for your head is worth a fortune. It could secure my place in the demon hierarchy." He took a couple of steps toward me, and I saw the road crack under his feet.

"Sorry, but that's not gonna happen," I retorted, launching myself at him, and unleashed a flurry of attacks. I flipped over and pitched my shurikens toward its neck, decapitating it. I stared on as its fell to the ground, lifeless. "Man, I'm getting too tough for these guys." I turned around to the hospital to check on the survivors when I was knocked over to the ground.

"Thought you got rid of me?" I turned to locate the voice and saw another stone demon standing right above me. I did a backflip and got back on my feet.

"So what are you?" I asked it. "The body I just destroyed is still on the ground. Are you a possessor? A cloning demon? What?"

"You will find out after you die, and I shall rip both souls from your body," It hissed. I began to brace for an attack when a white light shot through the top of its head to the ground. I watched as the creature peeled apart like a blooming flower.

"What the hell?" I looked at the center and saw, what looked like, a sword. It seemed to be glowing in a weird pattern. I stepped closer to get a better look.

"Not another step, abomination!" A voice boomed from above. I looked up to see a figure cloaked in white floating down to grab the sword. Its face was covered by a knight's helmet, and its body had various patches of armor and wings larger than its body. It pointed the sword at me. "Your little hero game has gone on long enough."

"What game?" I spat out. "I didn't ask for any of this! I was born this way. My mother had faith in humanity and volunteered to be part of the team to save it."

"Humanity has no choice in this matter. It is his divine will that will choose who amongst them will be saved. Humans were not meant to fight this. The apocalypse has been foretold since ancient times." The angel acted as though it was a robot reading off a script. "Those who have been faithful to him have nothing to fear."

"That would only apply if the demons weren't working ahead of schedule!" I shouted back in frustration. "Why hasn't he taken his faithful now, then?"

"He is not required to answer to you, abomination," it replied robotically. "We are to hand over those who broke the pact."

"Can you not think for yourself?" I asked. "It feels like these answers are all from some giant script."

"Free will was given to humanity. We are to follow orders," it replied without emotion. "You are not meant to exist. You…" It started a speech when another demon behind it appeared out of the rubble. "I warned him…" It didn't notice the demon approaching behind it.

"Uh…" I tried to interrupt, but the angel held up his hand to silence me.

Just let it attack the angel, Tiamat suggested.

I can't do that, I argued.

Look, I've come to understand your compassion. It's possible he killed your family though. Do you really want to save their killer? He asked.

I…no…but. I wasn't sure how to respond. Could I really watch something get killed while I could stop it? I watched the demon get behind it and raise its fist to come hurling down on its head. Acting on instinct, I leaped into action. "Look out!" I yelled, pushing the angel out of the way. I caught the demon's fists midair. Then, I kicked it back and aimed another shuriken at its head. As soon as it became lifeless, two more appeared.

"This isn't your fight, abomination!" The angel flew forward and ripped through the demons in a single slash. I jumped in and killed one that had appeared behind him. The demons started appearing faster.

"Yeah, let's just ignore the fact I've saved your ass twice now!" I took out a couple more that had just appeared. "Is there no end to this?" I shouted as two more appeared.

"That is why humans shouldn't fight." The angel took out two more, just as another pair appeared. "Angels are blessed by the divine. We don't tire."

"Must be nice!" I said as I took out another one.

This is getting us nowhere fast. Tiamat, you haven't been hiding the ability to sense demons, have you? I inquired.

No, why? You're fighting them now, he answered with sass.

I'm not sure we are, I told him as I took out another one. *These things are appearing faster than we can kill them. They just go lifeless when we kill them too. No cry of pain or anything.*

Your point being? he asked, confused.

I think we are dealing with golems, I responded, dodging while the angel took out another couple.

Golems? he asked. *As in pawns made of clay? I guess that would explain some things. Even still, the summoner would have to have eye contact to keep summoning them during the fight.*

Exactly, I nodded. I grabbed one of the enemies and spun in a circle before hurling it away from the hospital. I took the moment while circling to look around for where he could be hiding. I saw a pair of eyes in the corner office of a building window. *There! The corner office on the top floor. It would provide a perfect view of the fight. He can summon without worry from there. That's gotta be it.*

So what to do about our fighting companion? he laughed.

"Hey!" I shouted at the angel. "I think I figured out how to stop the flood of enemies. If we just—"

"The fight will stop once the demons are all dead," the angel said, taking another out while two more appeared in its place. He leaped back and charged again, killing the two that had just spawned. "Then you and I will finish what we started." He slayed another that appeared.

Well, I tried. I shrugged and felt Tiamat chuckle. *Time to test my teleportation accuracy.* I aimed my thoughts and teleported just as a golem was about to strike me. I found myself in an empty office. Staring out the window was a thin, frail demon. He had one hand over another. The top had strings glowing with energy. He moved them like he was moving a puppet. He was scanning the battle scene and the alley where the hospital was located. "Looking for me?" I asked. He spun around, and his eyes grew wide.

"H-h-h-how? W-w-when did you? My plan was perfect," he stammered in fright.

"Oh please, like I wouldn't figure out what I was fighting was lifeless eventually." He got angry at that and shot out his hand. I threw a shuriken in it, and he retracted it back, shrieking in pain.

There's the shriek you said was missing, Tiamat said.

You make me sound like a sadist when you put it that way, I smiled. "All right, game's over. Come on." I launched at him, grabbing him, and he held the stump where his hand used to be.

"Where are you taking me?" It asked

"To prove a point to a stubborn angel," I replied, crashed through the window using the demon as a shield. As I fell, I threw the demon toward the angel and teleported to him to avoid injury. The angel instinctively slashed through the flying demon, and the remaining golems instantly dropped to the ground, falling apart.

"Did you just try to attack me?" The angel asked as I walked toward it.

"No, I proved I knew what I was talking about," I answered. "Look around, the enemy is gone. The creature you slashed through was the demon summoning them. We were fighting an endless horde."

"I see," He responded with that, and only that.

"Look, I don't know what you want me to do," I began. "I don't know what to call you. Do you have a name?"

"Michael." A short answer again.

"Fair enough," I said. "Look, Michael, I don't know what you want me to do. You want me to stop, and even if I listen, the demons are still looking for me. I don't think it's a wise idea to let the demons have a dragon's soul, and I don't really want to give them mine either."

"I have been told to give you a chance at redemption," he informed me. "*He* is aware you weren't given a fair chance. If I slay you with this blade, your soul will be sent instantly to His Grace. You will be reunited with your loved ones in everlasting peace."

If he is telling the truth, that is not a bad offer, Tiamat voiced.

"Did you kill my family?" I asked coldly.

"Angels only follow orders," he responded

"That's not what I asked. I asked if you had killed my family. You said, 'be reunited with them.' That means they are up there, and demons didn't take their souls." I prepped a shuriken. "I ask again, did you kill my family?"

"I was not the one who killed your family." I threw the shuriken in the opposite direction to get rid of it. "I will not lie to you though. An angel did kill them. He went against orders and killed them."

"You said angels just follow orders and that they have no free will." I was getting angry. "If that's true, then how is it possible what you told me had happened?"

"An angel who doesn't follow orders becomes fallen," Michael tried to explain. "The angel that slew your family was sent to ask questions, not murder them. He grew impatient that they would not help locate Loki. He hated that they wouldn't turn you over willingly. In a moment of heat, he slew them all. Since his weapon was divine, the souls went straight to His Grace."

"So where is the angel that slew them?" I asked through gritted teeth.

"As I said, angels who disobey orders become fallen as punishment. We cannot track them anymore. I can tell you that, normally, they become demons," he responded. "So what is your answer?"

"What would happen to Alex?" I asked.

"Your friend's fate is up to His Grace. It depends on how faithful he has been," he answered. "I've only been told to give *you* a chance at redemption. Everyone else had had a fair chance already, and their fates have been decided."

"Then, while I must thank you for the shot, my answer is no."

"Can I ask why?" he asked. "You have been given a chance to get out of the fight and join your family. Why would any human turn that down?"

"Two reasons," I sighed. "First, honestly, I want vengeance on the fallen angel who had killed my family in cold blood. I promise you, I will have that revenge too, even at the cost of my life and soul. It's not just revenge for me—that fallen angel had also hurt the only other being on this planet who I would gladly take a bullet for. He took my best friend's family from him too. I won't just let that go. That brings me to my second reason: I will not just abandon Alex. He and I have been through too much together for me to just leave him here. I won't let him experience, literally, hell on earth alone." I turned to face him. "So there's your answer."

"So be it. I will return to Him and let Him know your response." He began to fly off.

"One more thing, Michael," I said before he stopped to look back. "I know you told me that it is humanity's destiny for the apocalypse to happen, but I've been given a shot at stopping it. I swear to you, I *will* stop Beelzebub from starting this thing. I will not die by his hand."

"Then next time, we may be enemies. That depends on His will." I swear I saw him smile through the helmet at my comment. "Farewell for now, abomination." I watched as a white beam enveloped his levitated form, and he disappeared.

"Um, sir?" I turned to see the soldier I had saved limping toward me. "Thank you for saving me. I knew the reports about you being evil had to be false. It just didn't add up." He saluted me.

"You're welcome," I responded. "No need to salute me though, I am not military."

"I know, but I don't know what else to do to thank you,"

"You can thank me by telling me how everyone is doing inside."

"See for yourself." He pointed at the hospital, and I saw window upon window of hospital staff and patients cheering at my victory. I smiled internally.

"Thank you," I nodded. "Now if you don't mind, I need to get back to the base and talk to Cooshings some more."

"Yes, sir." He almost saluted again out of habit before stopping. "I will remain on watch here."

"That's fine, but please stay safe yourself." I turned my back and began walking away.

Are you sure you made the right choice? Tiamat asked.

When are you going to learn that I'm not sure of anything? I responded. *Now, what do you say we get back to the army base at school?*

Fine with me, Tiamat responded. *Don't you think Alex is going to be pissed at you when he finds out you didn't take a chance at eternal peace because you wanted to keep him safe?*

Yeah, I sighed out loud, *that's one conversation I am not looking forward to having.*

Chapter Eight

"We got *big* trouble!" Harmony came barging in, out of breath, while I was talking to Cooshings. The dread in her eyes made my stomach sink. "Alex has been stabbed, and I can't get to him."

"Let's go!" I ran out of the tent following Harmony ignoring the general's objections. "What happened?"

"We got the weapons here, like you told us, and as we pulled up, we found Megan standing outside the base. She told Alex she was sorry, and he said it didn't matter. He said sorry wasn't enough this time. She begged him to take a walk with her and try to talk things out, and he agreed. He told me to wait for you and that he would be back soon. I was suspicious and followed without them knowing. At the next block, Megan hugged Alex, and I heard him scream out. When they separated, I saw a knife in her hand and Alex clutching his side. She told him, 'We will be together again soon.' That's when a demon took Megan, and she went willingly away. I tried to run up and help him, but a force field formed around him." As we turned the corner, the force field came into sight. We could see Alex's body lying still. "I'm sorry."

"It's not your fault. Let's just save him," I said as I ran up and barged against the shield and was immediately thrown back.

"It looks like he's still breathing, but that's a lot of blood he's lying in," Harmony told me in panic.

"Stand back!" I ordered. I transformed and hurled a wave of shurikens at the field. When the dust settled, the field was still standing.

"It's no use, dragon!" I spun around and saw Beelzebub approaching. "That shield is tied to me. Only I can release it. Your friend's soul is ours." He laughed. "Unless—"

"Unless what?" I asked. I already knew the answer.

"You give me your soul, and I will allow your friend to get the treatment he needs. Can't guarantee he will live though. The cut is pretty bad."

"Deal," I answered without a second thought.

"Sam!" Harmony yelled out in shock.

"Look, Harmony, the only reason I keep fighting is for him. If he dies, I've got nothing else to live for. Don't fight me on this, please. The angels are helping in the fight now too. I'm sure you can carry on without me," I pleaded.

"Then we have a deal." He held up his staff and energy started emitting from it. "See you in hell, dragon!"

"Hold it!" I shouted, and the energy stopped.

"What?" he asked, annoyed.

"Force field first, so I see you have kept your end of the deal, and I can say goodbye." I demanded.

"What's to stop you from breaking your end of the deal and running?"

"I'm the good guy here for crying out loud!" I shouted in panic. I watched as the shield dissipated.

"You've got two minutes," he said as I ran to him. Harmony followed close behind me.

"Alex!" I cried as I got to him. I knelt beside him, undid my transformation, and grabbed his hand. "Hold on, man. You need to stay with us."

"Sam?" He opened his eyes and let a small smile show. "I knew you'd come for me. Megan…"

"I know." I smiled back. I saw him wince in pain. "You need to hold on, man. You gotta live for the both of us."

"What does that mean?" His eyes went wide. "Sam?"

"I'm sorry," I said, avoiding his eye. "A world without you isn't worth living. I had to. I couldn't risk it." I stood up and began walking back to Beelzebub. "Forgive me."

"You finished saying your goodbyes?" he sneered.

"Let's just get this over with," I said, closing my eyes and spreading my arms out wide, opening myself up to the attack.

"As you will soon find out, dragon, this is only the beginning." I heard him fire the beam from his staff. I braced for it and felt *nothing!* "What treachery is this?" I opened my eyes and saw the shadow crystal floating in front of me, blocking the beam.

Fight. I heard a voice other than Tiamat's. It came from the crystal. It was a voice I didn't recognize; yet, somehow, it sounded familiar. *This isn't the way. You must fight.*

"I don't know. I guess I'm immune as long as I'm alive." I smiled.

"Then the deal is off!" shouted Beelzebub. He waved his staff, and the shield reappeared, trapping Alex and Harmony.

"Don't worry about us!" Harmony yelled. "I swear I'll keep Alex alive. Take him down!"

"As you wish!" I shouted back and transformed.

"You've got no chance, dragon!" he hissed, charging at me. I dodged out of the way and attempted a roundhouse. He caught my foot and tried to throw me. I leaned back and did a backflip. Beelzebub let go and flew into the air, firing shots from his staff. I tried to roll out of the way, but the last one caught me.

"Arghh!" I clenched my shoulder in pain. Spinning around, I threw a shuriken at him. He grasped it in his hand and crushed it.

"I told you, dragon," he sniggered. "You have no chance!"

Well, brawn doesn't work, I thought quickly as he unleashed another barrage of shots. *Time to use my head.* I launched my shurikens at the shots. They exploded, and I used the smoke to swiftly teleport above him. I threw shurikens at his wings as he looked around. A couple of pieces flew off, and I slammed into him. I teleported back to the ground and saw him plummeting down, hitting the ground at top speed.

"You brat." He staggered as he stood up. "No one grounds me and lives. I didn't want to use this power, but you leave me with no choice!" He held up his staff in the air. "Souls of my victims, give me strength. I command you!" A white mist dissolved into the staff. To my horror, Beelzebub began to glow. I threw shurikens at him, and they dissolved before even making contact. He laughed and flew at me, too fast for me to keep track. Before I could react, he shot me with a blast from his staff at point-blank range. I went hurtling back, skidding to a stop next to the shield trapping my friends.

"SAM!" Harmony shouted as I struggled to get up, blood seeping from my abdomen.

Don't give in! Tiamat encouraged.

What else can I do? I asked, slipping back onto the ground.

"Sam!" I heard Harmony again in the back of my mind. "I stopped Alex's bleeding, but I need to get him somewhere to rest. That means you need to survive this. Alex still needs you."

She's right, vessel. No, not vessel, Sam. You've already done the impossible. Your enemy is using the souls he has taken from victims to power himself. He is scared. He took them away from the seal on hell. Now push! End him. Now!

You're right. I can do this. I nodded. *Thanks, my friend.* I focused on the shadow crystal. *Please, shadow crystal, give me more strength. I need to slay this demon, use my life, if you must. Please, give me your all!*

I felt a strange power surging through me.

"Is that the best you can do, boy?" Beelzebub asked as I heard him approach. "Then this is the end of our rivalry. Goodbye, dragon."

"Don't count me out just yet." I projected a shield, pushing his blow away. I stood up, and all the pain was gone. I looked at my stomach and saw the wound had healed. I looked down at my hands. I was glowing with black energy surrounding me.

"Just *die* already!" He brought the staff down to strike me, but I grabbed on to it. I felt the power flare in my hand, and I crushed his staff, turning it to dust. He jumped back and exclaimed, "This...this cannot be! Where did this power come from?"

"Don't underestimate the power of a dragon and human working together. Farewell, Beelzebub!" I used the energy churning around me and lunged myself forward, slicing him with my bare hands. He flew back immediately, clutching the wound I gave him.

"You got the best of me this time, dragon!" he hissed. "It won't happen again." He disappeared, hollering a "farewell for now" as he exited.

"Sam!" I heard Harmony shout and teleported immediately to their side as the shield vanished.

"How is he?" I asked, glancing at his unconscious form.

"Alive, just unconscious. He's lost a lot of blood," she answered. "I've got the bleeding stopped like I said before, but we need to get him back to the lab."

"Say no more." I looked at my arms and focused. Immediately, I felt my arms grow cold. "Hold on tight," I said as I lifted Alex into my arms while Harmony held my hand. I focused hard, and the next thing I knew, we were all in the medic bay of the lab. I grew weak suddenly after I placed Alex on the bed, dropping to my knees as my strength failed me. I faced Harmony who stood speechless. "Get him back in shape," I pleaded as I finally lost consciousness.

I opened my eyes, and I saw I was back where I made the pact with Tiamat. "Am I dead?" I asked as I walked around.

"No. I stopped it in time." I spun around and saw Tiamat in front of me.

"So this is the real you," I remarked, getting a real look at him for the first time. "Why am I here again then?"

"When you used the crystal to that extent, it actually used your life force as a weapon," he explained. "When you were glowing, that was your life. The black energy was the shadow crystal tapped into it. That's how your wound healed too. The crystal stole some of your life to heal it"

"So you're saying that if I would have kept fighting like that...," I started.

"If that fight went on for much longer, you would have died. As soon as it was over, I began to try and separate the crystal and you. Luckily, you had enough life to survive once separated," he finished.

"So what now?" I asked.

"Now, you rest," he said. "You are safe in the lab. Alex is safe. Take this time to rest. Gain your life back before you wake up."

"But—" I hesitated.

"No debating," he ordered. "I don't know if I can save you next time. The fight still continues, and you *must* regain your strength. Beelzebub is gravely injured, but not gone."

"Fine," I relented. "Is there someone else in the crystal?"

"Not that I am aware of. Why do you ask?"

"When I was ready to give myself up to save Alex, I heard a voice. It told me that giving up wasn't the way and that I had to keep fighting."

"Maybe it was the crystal itself."

I was stunned. "Is that possible?"

"Legend has it that when the crystal was whole, it had a spirit residing within it," he explained. "Maybe a part of that spirit survived the split."

"I guess that's possible," I yawned. "So how exactly do I rest? Pure white light isn't exactly easy to sleep with."

"Reach into the darkness again," he said, and with that, he turned into the dark sphere I had originally seen. Without hesitation, I reached in. Darkness consumed me, and my consciousness faded.

Chapter Nine

"Alex!" I sprang awake and found myself sitting up in bed at the medical bay.

Harmony walked into the room smiling. "He's in the bed next to you." I turned to see Alex in the bed hooked up to monitors. "Nice to see you awake finally. How do you feel?"

"Honestly?" I questioned, and she nodded. "Hungry," I declared.

"Well, I guess that's to be expected," she laughed. "You've been out for two weeks."

"No attacks?" I asked.

"Nothing that the military couldn't handle with our weapons. Cooshings asked where you went. I told him, after dealing major damage to the enemy, you fell into a coma," she explained. "I told him you would return once you woke up. He wishes you well."

"I bet he does." I rolled my eyes. "And Alex?" I looked down at his sleeping figure.

"I don't know. I'm sorry." She looked dejected. "I can't see anything wrong medically. His blood count is back up, he's got no fever, and the stab wound has almost completely healed. He just won't wake up." She and I sat in silence for a minute. "I'm going to find you something to eat. When I come back, I'll tell you what I have discovered about the sword you want to find." With that, she left me to my own thoughts. I went and sat down next to Alex, holding his hand.

*Tiamat, you don't think his soul...*I couldn't bring myself to finish.

No. If he had lost his soul, he would be completely dead, he answered. I sighed with relief.

"I'm sorry, Alex," I mumbled. "If I hadn't asked you to get the weapons, you wouldn't have seen Megan, and you wouldn't be lying here now fighting for your life." I brought his hand to my forehead with both my hands and closed my eyes. "You *need* to wake up. You *need* to get through this. I still need you."

"You two really are close," Harmony expressed as she walked back in and handed me a bag of chips. "I'm kind of jealous."

"He means everything to me." I opened the bag and stuffed my mouth quickly. "If he doesn't come back from this, I swear I..."

"He will." She put her hands on mine. "If there is one thing I've learned about the two of you over this short period of time is that the bond you two have makes you unbeatable. He will get over this and get back to you. You've just got to keep faith."

"Thanks." I popped my back sitting there, forcing myself not to cry. "So the sword?" I asked, changing the subject.

"Right," she smiled. "There is a myth that I kept finding, of a sword hidden away somewhere within an Aztec temple in a hidden village."

"Great! So that narrows it down to a whole country," I jeered, rolling my eyes.

She gave me a sly smile. "That's what I thought too at first."

"At first?" I raised an eyebrow. "You got something else then?"

"Who do you think you are talking to?" she said with mocked anger. "I figured that, in order to slay demons, it had to be blessed by someone holy. And who's holier than the Pope?" She pulled out her laptop and opened a mapping program. "I looked up all known routes previous popes had taken while in Mexico. Notice anything?" I watched the program run. It traced all the routes out.

"What's up with this one?" I asked, noticing one pope had ventured out of his way for one day before returning to the regular routes the others had taken.

"Exactly." She nodded. "Every other pope took the same route. This one went out of his way to visit this small village. I'm betting the hidden temple lies somewhere in this area." She highlighted the area between the stops before and after the isolated village.

"So the best bet is to head to the first village and follow the route," I suggested.

"Why not head to the isolated village, look, and ask for clues?"

"One problem with that."

"What's that?"

"I don't speak Spanish." I shrugged. "And I'm guessing, in an isolated village, people speaking English will be hard to come by."

"That makes sense." She nodded. "All right, so I got to ask then, what language *do* you have for the graduation credit?"

"Japanese," I answered with a smile.

"When are you going to use that?" She laughed.

"When I have to kick some demon butts in Tokyo," I answered back, annoyed.

"Yeah, *now* maybe, but—"

"Look, let's just move on." I shot her a glare, and she shut up. "All right, do you have an image of a secluded spot in the first city? Preferably recent."

"I can look one up real quick. Why?"

"When I teleport, I have to have a visual of my destination in mind," I explained. "Since I've never been there, I need a picture to try and use."

"How's this?" She held the laptop up, which displayed the village entrance from behind some bushes. "Real-time photo, so it should be accurate."

"Hopefully this works then." I studied it and nodded. "I've never teleported off a picture before." I stood back and transformed, wobbling a little bit.

"Take it easy, there is no rush. If you are not healed fully, then wait," she pleaded.

"There is a rush though." I tried to point out. "The only reason there have been no major attacks is because Beelzebub is too weak from our fight to send the big demons through whatever opening he has. I need the sword before he can heal enough to start sending strong demons again."

"Fine," she huffed. "There is something else you should know about the legends behind this sword: the sword is supposedly cursed. Every legend I read said that anyone whoever had touched it has killed themselves with it."

"Makes sense since it can kill angels." I sighed when I saw the worried look on her face. "Look, I'll be fine. It's not just me who's going to control it. I have Tiamat's help too. I promise I won't touch it without being transformed." I held up my right hand as I said it.

She looked away. "I still worry. Believe it or not, I think of you as a friend."

"I think of you as one as well." I tried to think of something to help. "Look, if you're worried, just make sure Alex gets better. He has talked me out of losing myself before. If anyone can keep me sane, it's him."

"I'll do what I can." She nodded. "I just can't find anything wrong."

"I'm sure you will figure it out." I stood up and went to the center of the room. "When he wakes up, if I'm not back, get him up to speed." She nodded. I looked at the picture, mumbled a silent prayer for safety, and teleported.

"*Monstrou!*" I heard upon landing behind some trees. I turned to see a Hispanic middle-aged man shaking while staring at me.

"Easy there," I said, holding up my hands to try and calm him down. "I'm not going to…" I stepped on a twig, and its snap was apparently like a gunshot to the frightened man.

"*Monstrou!*" his voice echoed behind him as he bolted toward the village.

Well, that went well, Tiamat teased.

Shut up, I shot back. I saw guards approaching the man, and he pointed back toward me. *Time to go.* I launched myself into the nearby woods and kept going until the village was at least a mile behind me.

You didn't have to run, Tiamat laughed.

Look, I just wanna find the sword, I answered, walking through the trees. *I'd rather not make waves in these people's lives.*

Chicken, he snickered.

*Not a chic...*I tripped and went rolling down a steep hill, smacking against a tree to stop....*ken. Ow.* I rubbed my side.

That's my vessel! Able to defeat any demon, bested by a tree. He was rolling in my head by now.

Damn, you're feisty today. What's up with you? I asked as I dusted myself off.

Honestly, I don't know. I've felt this way ever since we arrived, he replied.

Maybe you are getting sick, I suggested. *Can souls even get sick?*

Good question, he admitted. *This is all new to me too.*

*We will have to ask the professor when we get...*I stopped my thought as I reached a clearing. On the other side, I could see a ruined village. The buildings had all but collapsed, and every building except one was almost completely knocked over. At the center of the village was an ornate temple, and it appeared well-kept. I walked toward it and noticed it appeared to be made of solid gold. *back,* I finished my thought. *I think we may have found the sword.*

Let's hurry up then, I felt his panting. *I suddenly feel really weird.*

It's probably the sword, I reasoned. I walked up to the temple entrance. *It is cursed after all.* I pushed the golden doors open and tasted the stale air. *I just hope both of us together is enough to keep it from controlling us.*

As I stepped in, I leaped as the door slammed shut behind me. At the back of the room were stairs leading to an altar. The altar had intricate carvings, and on top, was a sword. As I began to climb the stairs up to the blade, torches on either side of me began to light themselves. *Well, this is spooky.* I reached the top and examined the blade. The sheath was pitch black and the hilt was gold. The handguard seemed to be made almost entirely of some kind of bone. I took a deep breath and grabbed the sword, was instantly flung back to the center of the room. I watched, on guard, as the room filled with a white mist.

"You've done well finding this place," a voice called out from the mist. I got up and readied for battle, holding the sword in front of me. "Stand down, young dragon, I mean you no harm."

My grip tightened. "Sorry, but I find that hard to believe when I'm talking to thin air."

"Well, let's talk face-to-face then." As soon as the voice said that, a figure, cloaked in darkness, appeared in front of me. I jumped back to give myself distance. "I am the demon that resides in the sword you now hold."

"Great! An opportunity to test this then." I smirked and lunged at him. He jumped back and held out his hand; the blade grew unbearably heavy.

"As I said before, I mean you no harm." He brought his hand back into the shadows as I struggled to lift the blade. "I do, however, wish for a chance to talk to you."

Vessel…are…you…what…on? Tiamat's voice struggled to get through.

"So this is in my head, huh?" I smirked.

"Yes and no," he answered. He waved his hand, and Tiamat's presence vanished. "That's better." I looked down and found that I was human again. "Now that we have no interruptions—"

"What did you do to Tiamat?" I yelled, getting angry.

"I simply blocked his communication with you. As you said yourself, this is in your head. Only I am in control." He snapped his fingers, and we were no longer in the temple, but a cave-like environment. "Ah, home sweet home." He took his seat on a stone in the corner.

"How can you control what's in my mind?" I asked.

"I can do a lot more than that." He smirked. "With your help."

I still tried to lift the sword. "What do you mean with my help?"

"Before that foolish pope helped that witch trap me in this sword, I came across a legend: a human, with the power of light and dark, will be born. When he is born, and if he comes into his full power, he will be able to reshape the world as he sees fit." He then pointed at me. "And now that child has been born."

"I think you have the wrong child," I shot back. "Yes, Tiamat was born of the dark dragon clan, but I don't have the power over it and much less power over light."

"That's where I come in. You see, when the pope blessed the sword to trap me, he had accidentally blessed me as well." He got in my face, and I saw that a part of it looked almost human. "I have since learned how to control the powers he had blessed me with. Join with me, accept me into your soul. Together, we will have power over the earth. We will be gods!"

"Yeah, and why would I just abandon everyone I know?" I asked, thinking of Harmony and Alex.

"You want to see your family again, right?" All of a sudden, he assumed the shape of my dad. "If you join him"—my "dad" said before the figure became my mom—"we can be together again. Don't you want that?" she asked. "You will have the power to bring us back to life. Don't you want that?" She rubbed my hair, and I dropped to my knee. "We could be one big happy family again."

"But, Alex," I began to lose touch with sanity and tried to focus on my friend. "He's hurt. I need to get back to him."

"Leave him." My "mom" hissed and then composed herself. "You heard the demon. This is your chance to become a *god*. Forget about your friend. He has outlived his usefulness anyway. I agreed to do the experiment so that you could survive. With this chance, you could do more than that. You could rule the universe. You can make Mommy proud!" The way she talked about Alex snapped me back to reality. I focused on the shadow crystal and saw that it was still there. I prayed for its power.

"Only one problem," I said, feeling like my old self again.

"What's that, darling?" She walked up close to me again. I tapped into the crystal, freeing the sword from whatever the demon had done to make it heavy. I stabbed it into the image of my mother in the heart with my tears flowing freely.

"You're not my mother!" I shouted, taking the blade out and watched as the image flashed back into the demon.

"H-How?" He fell to his knees, clutching the wound. "It's not possible. No one can break my control."

"My mom would never tell me to betray my friends. Loyalty is everything." I dragged the sword across the ground and brought it up to the demon. It split in half before vanishing entirely. I dropped to my knees and began sobbing.

What happened, vessel? I heard Tiamat's voice again and noticed I was back in the real world, still transformed. I was still holding the blade that was on my knees. I kept crying. *Vessel? Sam? What happened? You froze up, and I couldn't snap you out of it. Next thing I know, you're on the ground in tears.*

Later, I answered, gathering myself before standing. *I just want to get home and check on Alex.* I tried to teleport but wound up on the same spot in the altar. *That was weird. Why can't I teleport?*

Perhaps the demon of the sword, Tiamat offered.

I killed the demon. The curse of the sword is no more.

How? When? he asked, confused.

When I froze up, that was him invading my mind, I answered. *I'll tell you all about it later, but I want to go home.*

If it's not the demon, maybe it's the temple, he tried again. *This place was built to trap the demon, right? Maybe it has the ability to block our power to leave too somehow.*

That's as good a theory as any. Let's go outside and try again. I nodded and walked out the temple doors.

"So the mighty dragon has managed to survive even the Masamune curse." A voice boomed as soon as I stepped into the sunlight. I spun around, looking for the voice. "I'm impressed." I looked on top of the temple and found an angel standing there. "You might even be stronger than the rumors I've heard." He jumped down and landed in front of me.

"Look, I've already had a long day. I really don't want to fight an angel now too," I pleaded, hoping he would just go away.

"That's good. I'm no angel," he smirked as he drew his sword and pointed it at me. "At least, not anymore."

"What do you mean?" I got that sinking feeling and got ready to fight.

"I stopped being an angel the day I decided to slaughter your family," he said as he thrust himself at me.

Chapter Ten

"Foolish humans didn't know what kind of powers they were toying with!" he spat as I defended myself. I countered, and he jumped back. "It was pure joy watching them beg as I tortured them until they were lifeless!"

"You bastard!" I cried, thrusting myself at him till our swords collided. I struggled to overpower him. "Why? From what Michael said, you weren't supposed to *kill* them."

"Ah, Michael, the Lord's perfect little soldier, blindly following orders." He flapped his wings once, and I went flying back. "I did it for power. My plan was to kill you and take the dragon soul for myself. Your parents wouldn't talk in time though. God noticed what I was doing and sent Michael to clip my wings, exiling me to this shitty area." He flapped his wings again, but I braced myself this time. When I opened my eyes, he was in striking distance. I brought my sword up and blocked. "As luck would have it, I found this place. I knew if I waited, you would too, and I was right. Here you are, walking straight to your death."

"Sorry, but I don't plan on dying." I spun away from the lock and fired a couple shurikens at him. They hit him, and he laughed.

"The thing about me is, while I may be fallen, I am still an angel." I watched wide-eyed as the wounds from my shurikens healed themselves. "Your dragon powers will do you no good in this fight." He held up his hands, and the wind literally began to tear at my skin.

I screamed and hit my knee. "However, my remaining angelic powers will work wonders on you."

Teleport away! Tiamat urged. *You can't win this right now. We need to regroup.*

I won't run. He murdered my family. I stood up and prepared to strike. *I will strike him down, even if it's the last thing I do.*

"That's it, give into your hatred." He cackled. "It will make you an easy kill." He whipped up the wind again.

"I won't fall as easy as you think." I threw shurikens into the dirt, and with the wind he whipped up, they started a major dust cloud. I teleported behind him and did the same thing when he tracked me. The dust had completely surrounded him at this point.

"Think you can blind me for an advantage?" he called out. "I can blow this away with ease." He took his attention off me for a split second and blew the dust away. I took that chance to drop in from above. He noticed me just as I came within striking distance. Before he could react, I cut off his arm.

"Well, I guess the rumors of this blade having demonic powers is true, huh?" I couldn't help but grin as he clutched the bleeding stump and cried out in pain. Pretty soon, his cry turned into a crazy cackle.

"I never would have dreamed you could hurt me." He his cackle continued. I watched in awe as his pure white wings grew black-edged, and his face gained black patterns around it. "Lord Beelzebub was right. Your power is remarkable. I must have it. Even if it means using the demonic gift he had offered me."

Why is there always a phase two? I watched as a tentacle-like vine grew out of the stump where his arm used to be, and a black aura enveloped his body. The vine plunged at me. I sliced a part of it off, but it kept growing back. I jumped out of the way and began dodging the vine as it came after me.

"How long can you keep this up, dragon?" he laughed as I sliced through an enclosed path. I kept dodging, all the while trying to figure out what to do. I looked up and noticed he had trapped us in a cage with his vines. I was quickly running out of options. I tried to jump up toward the roof of the cage, but his vine caught my foot before I could reach the exit. He pulled me back to the ground.

"Crap!" I couldn't help but cry out as I hit the ground with a thud. I heard him laughing as he twirled me around like a ragdoll. He finally threw me against the temple wall and used his vines to hold me in place.

"HAHAHA!" he broke out in a wicked laugh. "Soon, I will be the ultimate being." He approached me, and I struggled to free myself. "As soon as I have the dragon soul under my control, no one, not even God himself, can stop me." I began to grow numb; my circulation was cut off.

I'm sorry, Tiamat. I closed my eyes and braced for the end. *You were right, I was blinded by my rage.*

I would have done the same in your shoes. You are the one who taught me about strategy, he replied. *Let me at least seal your soul in the shadow crystal, so it doesn't get lost to the demons.* I began to feel a warmth as Tiamat began to take over.

"What is the meaning of this?" the angel cried out.

Tiamat, stop! I cried out. *I feel someone is trying to help us.* I opened my eyes to see the vines glowing red above us. I heard the sound of something hitting it.

"What are you doing?" he spat at me, turning his watchful eyes from me to the glowing vines above. I saw a brief flash of fear come across his face.

"It's not me," I answered. I watched as there was a sudden explosion. The vines above us burnt to a crisp as a fireball came flying at us. The angel stepped out of the way as the fireball landed next to me, and a human-like form emerged from it. It stepped toward the angel and threw its arms at him. Flames engulfed the angel, and I heard him screaming in pain as the flames held him at bay.

"Are you all right?" it asked as it ran up to me and grabbed the vines encasing me; they instantly dissolved to ashes. It held out a hand for me to grab and helped pull me up to my feet.

"Yeah, thanks to you," I replied.

"Good. Although I should have left you there for a while longer."

"Why is that?" I asked, trying to figure this new creature out and why it appeared so familiar.

"Because you keep breaking your promises to me," it answered. I gasped, suddenly realizing why it felt so familiar.

"Alex?" I shouted, and he nodded. "How? What? When?" I scrambled to make sense of what I was seeing. The flaming creature with wings really was my best friend.

"Kill now, talk later." He pointed to our fallen angel friend trapped in the ball of flames. I stepped forward and nodded.

"I won't be defeated by you half-breeds!" he screamed and broke free from the flames. The flames came at me as he struggled to stand. Alex ran up and stood in front, letting the flames strike him.

"I told you," I answered, stepping beside Alex again. "I won't die so easily, but now it's time to end this!"

"Let's finish him, Sam!" Alex cried out. "I'll cover you from above." I watched as he flapped his wings and hovered above me.

"I am Lucifer II, the greatest force and will be the next God of all!" he cried out and sent the vines flying at us. I brought up my sword to defend, but a wall of flames appeared in front me.

"Sam, now!" Alex ordered. I nodded and stormed toward Lucifer II, my sword in hand. Alex flew in from above and pushed the fire wall to intercept any vines that came our way.

"Impossible!" Lucifer cried out as we approached him.

"Check again," I jeered as I held my sword out to strike. "This is for our families. Goodbye!" I reached out through the fire wall and sliced his head off. I watched the head roll away from Lucifer's body as it collapsed lifeless.

"Our families?" Alex asked, landing next to me.

I turned to Alex and undid my transformation before dropping to my knees. "He was the one."

"Then that's why?"

"Yeah, that's why I kept fighting. That's why I didn't teleport to safety. I just kept thinking of my mom and dad dying as he stood over them laughing." I looked up at him and began to sob. "I'm sorry."

"For what?"

"I wasn't strong enough. Even with the sword, even with Tiamat helping me, I wasn't strong enough. If you hadn't shown up when you did, I would have left you alone," I sobbed. "Then again, if Beelzebub had his way that night, I would have left you alone then too."

"It's okay now. It all worked out." He came running to embrace me, undoing his transformation in the process. "We were strong enough—together."

"But…" I sobbed onto his shoulder.

"No buts. Look at me," he comforted. "I promised you. We will get through this *together*. We were strong enough then, and we will be in the future. *Together* we will overcome your destiny." He smiled. "Besides, I should be apologizing to you."

I began to breathe normally. "Why?"

"You warned me of Megan, and I knew she was mad. I could never imagined she'd make a deal with a demon just to have me." He looked hurt. "You should have never been put in the position to offer your soul in exchange for mine." He enveloped me in a big bear hug.

"So guessing we are still good then?"

"Always!" was his reply.

"Good because as much as I love your hugs, can you let me go now?" I chuckled. "Having a little trouble breathing." He immediately let go of me, and we both shared a good laugh. "So what was that little display of power? Last time I checked, I was the only one with a transformation."

"Well, don't be mad," he began.

"Spill it!" I demanded.

"Well, when you told Harmony to stop the bleeding, she was having issues. She told me she had one more option, but needed my approval. The professor had found a vial that was the essence of a phoenix soul. He gave it to Harmony and told her to use it only if she was about to die. The phoenix's soul has the power to heal the wounded. She told me she was willing to give it to me, but she had no idea what the side effects, if any, there would be."

"You had her inject you then?" I asked, already knowing the answer from the last battle.

"I couldn't just leave you alone. We made a promise to each other, remember?" He smiled.

I looked away. "Yeah, one that I was willing to break to save you."

"No, one that I was about to force you to break. I don't blame you, dude," he said as I turned back.

"So you have a phoenix soul in you now?"

"No, not exactly," he replied. "From what I can gather, all I was injected with the essence of one. I don't have the voice in my head like you do. I guess I gained the powers of one though, so I'm no longer the helpless damsel in distress." He threw his hand over his forehead, and we both laughed out. "Seriously though, now I can help you in your fight."

"I just don't want you to get hurt again," I pleaded.

"I'll be fine, I promise. See this?" He lifted his shirt to show where he was stabbed. "Not even a scar."

"I'm not gonna be able to convince you otherwise, am I?"

"Nope." He shook his head and threw his arm over my shoulder. "You are just stuck with me."

"I guess there are worse things in the world," I teased. "Seriously though, I'm just glad you're okay. I don't know what I would do if I lose you."

"You would move on and find someone else." He laughed before I slapped him on the head.

"I'm serious," I scowled.

"Oh, come on, quit dreading of stuff from the past." He smiled at me. "I'm fine, and you're fine. The here and now, that's all that matters. If we worry about the past, we won't want to fight for the future."

"I guess you're right," I mumbled. "So shall we get back to the lab and let them know the mission was a success? And I have what I need to kill Beelzebub?"

"Sounds like a plan." He nodded.

"You want a lift?" I asked, transforming.

"Yes, please." He nodded. "While I can fly home, somehow it's just not as fast as teleporting." He smiled and grabbed my shoulder, and together, we teleported back to the lab.

Chapter Eleven

"Burn baby burn!" Alex laughed maniacally. I rolled out of the way and threw a shuriken at him. He hurled fire at it, and it exploded, blinding us both. I lunged at him, but he was ready and caught my fist. "Don't you know I know all your tricks?"

"Not all of them," I smirked. "Look at my other hand." He followed my arm and noticed I was holding my sword against his stomach.

"Damn! I almost had you that time." He let me go and turned back to his human form. "Since when did you start using the sword with your left hand?" He asked, wiping sweat with a towel.

"Since you almost started beating me," I admitted. "I can't really fight with it in that hand, but its good enough to use for a fatal blow if I need to. Gotta keep you on your toes." I dodged the towel he threw at me.

"You boys done training in here yet?" Harmony appeared in the doorway with a tray of food in her hands.

"Food!" Alex cheered, running up to her.

"I think what Alex means is 'thank you.'" I laughed, watching Alex devour the plate of food in front of him. "What the hell, man? You not gonna save me any?"

"Sorry, man." He shrugged. "You know how hungry I get when I'm training, and now that I'm exerting myself in new ways, I'm even hungrier."

I rolled my eyes and laughed as he flipped me off. "Oh joy, lucky me."

"That's why I hid the other tray." Harmony laughed and revealed another tray of food which I eagerly accepted.

"You're the best." I smiled, biting into the hamburger.

"I know," she puffed out her chest and nodded. "Don't forget you have a meeting with Cooshings later."

"I know. I plan on cleaning up after I eat," I affirmed. "Still, why do you think it's been so quiet lately?"

"That's something to discuss when Cooshings is here."

"I still can't believe the professor is letting him come here," Alex piped in. "I thought this place was kind of like our secret headquarters."

"I think it's clear that I am not an enemy to them." I shrugged. "Besides, here we have an advantage if they try something else."

"If we wanted to try something, you would be dead." Mathers appeared next to Harmony in the doorway.

"Thanks for the heads-up, Harmony." I choked on my bite as she laughed.

"When you guys are ready, the professor and the general are in the surveillance room," Mathers informed before walking away.

"Well, ain't he just a bundle of fun?" Alex mocked, and I couldn't help but snicker.

"I better follow him," Harmony said rolling her eyes and turned to walk away. "I will see you guys in there." She waved before following Mathers out.

I took the last bite of my burger and set my plate down. "Come on."

"What about your fries?" Alex asked.

"If you want them, they're yours. Let's just get ready!" I shouted back. I was halfway down the hall already.

"Thanks!" Alex came bolting after, the plate in his hand. "So how do you think this meeting is going to go?" he asked between bites.

"How should I know?" I returned while going through the bag I had brought with me to grab a clean shirt. "I mean, I would think okay. It's been real quiet, so I think this is mainly going to be a meeting to prepare for a disaster."

"I know," Alex added while putting on his clean shirt. "It's just that we still are real tense around each other. I can't imagine that it will go perfectly smooth."

"I'd rather relations be tense than volatile," I said. "It's just nice not being considered public enemy number one anymore."

"I get it man," Alex responded. "So, between you and me, do you think Beelzebub is planning something?"

"There's not a doubt in my mind. He's up to something, and I've just got to be ready for it...whatever it is."

"It's not just you anymore, remember?" Alex grabbed my hand. "*We* have to be ready."

"You're right. I just don't want anything to happen to you." I sighed, walking toward the surveillance room.

"Will you quit that already? I told you it won't." He put his hand on my shoulder as he caught up. "I promise you, I'm not going anywhere." We reached the door, and Alex asked, "You ready for this?" I nodded, and we walked in.

"Glad to see you are feeling better," General Cooshings said as I walked in.

"Yup. I am a hundred percent again." I nodded.

"So are you ready to join us and go on the offensive?" he asked.

"You ask that like you have a way to follow the demons into hell," the professor added.

"We believe we are close to that, yes," Cooshings replied.

All of the sudden, the whole place began to quiver, and the alarms started going off.

"What's going on?" Mathers barked.

"There's a demon somewhere in town," the professor informed as he and Harmony ran to the keyboards and started punching numbers.

"Yeah, but last time it did this and I was here, the room wasn't shaking!" Alex pointed out.

"I'm working on it!" Harmony shouted as she typed frantically.

"I don't like this. I have a really bad feeling right now," I said. "I think this is what Beelzebub was waiting on."

"This can't be right," Harmony said, her voice full of panic. "Dad?"

"I hear you, Harmony," he responded. "Pulling up the video footage."

We all turned to the cameras. Demons were on a rampage all over the city.

"It's like an alien invasion!" Mathers said as we watched frightened civilians fleeing in terror.

"That means there's a 'mother ship' somewhere," I said. "Harmony, any luck?" I asked, noticing she was still typing.

"Yeah, but it's not good," she said with sheer dread in her eyes. "Look at the main display. I'm pulling it up right now." The monitor blinked over, and it showed demons pouring out of a medieval castle.

"Where is that?" Cooshings asked.

"The city lake," she answered.

"How? Last time I checked, there was no castle there," Alex pointed out. "And it's only two in the afternoon, but it's pitch black there."

She continued to stare in disbelief. "I don't know how to explain it, but that's definitely the lake there."

"All right, so we know where the source is, but does anyone have any ideas?" I asked. "Even if Alex and I separated, there are too many demons out already to prevent mass murder. That also won't stop demons from pouring out the castle to replace what we kill."

"Leave the demons in town to my men," Cooshing said, hanging up a phone I never noticed him using.

"Are you sure?" I asked.

"Yeah, they have gotten good at fighting these little guys." Cooshing nodded. "We just need to find a way to at least cut back on what's pouring out and get the two of you inside."

"If you're sure," I said, and he nodded. "All right then, anyone have a plan how to get us in that castle?"

The professor spoke up. "Actually, I do."

"Dad, are you sure?" she asked. "We haven't even had the chance to run any tests on it yet."

"It's all we have, and you know it," he stated. Harmony sighed and nodded, relenting.

"Someone want to fill us in?" asked Alex.

The professor walked out the door. "Follow me. I'll explain on the way." We all followed him out, turning down a corridor I've never been through before. "Ever since all this began, I figured it would come down to a situation like this. I've been working on a weapon that will protect the people inside and be capable of taking on hundreds of enemies while moving."

"So you've been working on a tank?" Cooshing asked, and Mathers snickered.

"Yes and no," he answered, glaring at Mathers who shut up. "Every tank I've ever seen moves slowly. I built this with a special alloy I had developed. It can even keep up with a jet, but it can also take a hit like any top-of-the-line tank out there." We stopped at a garage door where he pressed a button, and the door began to open. "Gentlemen, I would like to introduce you to the Automatic Demon Annihilation Machine, or ADAM for short."

"I'm actually impressed," Mathers expressed. ADAM was huge; it looked like it could comfortably fit in at least fifteen people, like a camouflaged metal space shuttle. There was a ramp in front to get in, and above it was a giant gun.

"It's even better inside." He held out what looked like car keys and hit a button. The door on the other side of the ramp opened with a whoosh. "After you, guys." He motioned for us to pass him and walk into ADAM.

Cooshing gawked around as he sat down in the driver's seat and ran his hands over the dashboard. "Wow, this is way better than anything we own."

"You installed leather seats since I've been here last," Harmony said, bouncing up and down in a side chair.

"Is that a mini fridge?" Alex asked.

"Fully stocked," the professor nodded. I watched Alex run for it and grab a couple of sodas. He came back and tossed one to me. Mathers went up to the driver's seat and looked around.

"What kind of heat are we packing?" He looked around. "I don't see anything."

"That's upstairs," Harmony said, smiling. "Follow me." We went upstairs and came face-to-face with two machine guns and a cannon. "These babies will tear the horde demons to shreds." She patted one and added, "They run off a synthetic soul generator I had developed. This means that, as long as the generator's running, you can keep shooting."

"Infinite ammo," Mather said, and I could swear I saw some drool come out. "I call dibs on one of the guns."

"So what's the plan?" I asked, ignoring him.

"I think our best bet is that the General and I pilot this to the lake. Harmony and Mathers will man the guns, and you two will prepare to launch an assault at the castle once we create an opening for you," the professor suggested.

"Works for me!" Mathers jumped excitedly into the gunner's seat.

"Let's move then if everyone's okay with this. The longer we debate, the more demons are going to come through," I said, and everyone nodded. Harmony went and took a seat next to Mathers. The rest of us went downstairs.

"All right, General, why don't you drive, and I copilot?" the professor suggested, and the general nodded.

"That makes sense," he said, taking a seat behind the wheel. "I have no clue what any of these buttons do."

"So how do we get this baby to the surface?" Alex asked as they started the engines.

103

"We just ride up and out," came the professor's answer. He pressed a button on the dashboard, and we lifted up and out on a lift. We exited right where I had saved Harmony that day. "Hang on tight, everyone, here we go." He hit another button, and we were launched forward.

Alex came and placed his hand on my shoulder. "How are you holding up?"

"About as well as I can be, I suppose." I looked back at him and smiled. "I mean, this is it! The whole world is counting on me. If I can't do this, if I die here, then…"

"You can do this," he reassured me. "You have already constantly surprised everyone. Between your brain and Tiamat's strength and powers, you can defy all odds. Don't forget you're not alone in this. These guys will make sure we get in, and then you have me."

"Just be sure to keep yourself safe." I leaned into him. "I don't know what I would do if anything happens to you during this—" We hit a bump, and he caught me.

"Same goes for you, man," he laughed and set me upright. "This will work out. You will kill Beelzebub, and we will both get to move on with our lives."

"Guys, hate to break up the pep talk, but you need to look at this!" the professor shouted. We ran to the window and looked out. The park in front of the lake was like a sea of horde demons scattered in different directions. At the center of the lake, a castle now stood with flying demons surrounding it.

"Wow! We got here fast," Alex said.

"Like a jet, remember?" The professor smiled.

"Guys, not the time to joke," I scolded, and both looked ashamed. "We are seriously outnumbered here. Even with the guns going, I don't know how we can get to the front door." A loud screech caught our attention, and we turned back to see the horde demons heading our way.

"I think they spotted us!" Harmony shouted as she and Mathers opened fire. I watched as they held the line but couldn't push them back further.

"This is pointless. They are sending out just as many as we are killing. We won't be able to reach Beelzebub at this rate," I said, starting to panic.

"Breathe, dude," Alex said, shaking me. "There has to be a way, and we just haven't thought of it yet." I took deep breaths, calming down. I looked around outside and racked my brain for anything, any chance to make it inside. I looked at Alex, and an idea struck me.

"How tired did that flame wall make you before?" I asked.

"Not tired at all," he answered. "The flames are just second nature. Why?"

"Can you put a box around me?" I asked. Alex caught on and nodded.

"Think it will work?" he asked. "What about the fliers? I would be a sitting duck for them."

"Hey, Harmony!" I shouted, running up the stairs.

"Kind of busy right now," she said as she kept shooting. "What's your plan?"

"If we fire the cannon right in front of the tank, will that push them back enough for us to get out?" I asked

"I suppose. Why?" she asked.

"Here is the plan then," I started, mouthing a quick prayer that it would work, "we fire the cannon, and Alex and I bail out of here. Alex, you place a fire cube around me, and we make a run for the front door. Once we do that, the majority of the demons would come after us, and Mathers should be able to defend the tank. Harmony, switch to shooting the flying demons out of the sky, so Alex can fly safely. Once we get to castle, you guys can escape and help the other officers around the city."

"One problem with that," Alex said. "How do we get inside once we get to the door? The demons are still pouring out of it."

"I admit the plan is flawed." I nodded. "We are just going to have to improvise."

The professor came up the stairs behind us. "I can help with that," he said, holding up a small bottle glowing in multiple colors. He grabbed something off a shelf, which appeared to be a rocket launcher or something. "Fire this at the doorway once you get there," he said, loading the glowing bottle into it. "It should create an opening for you to get inside."

"What is it?" Alex asked.

"It's basically a volatile cocktail of soul remains," he answered. "When I first began to experiment with souls, I found out that what I didn't use became unstable. I found a way to bottle it and save it for an emergency."

"Is it safe?" Harmony asked.

"Is any of this safe?" he asked back, and I shrugged, taking the weapon. "Look, it's not a guarantee, and I'm not going to lie, it may backfire and kill us all."

I sighed and took it. "It's still our best bet though."

"You sure, man?" Alex asked, and I nodded and transformed. He followed suit.

"Ready when you are," I said, and Alex nodded at me. "Professor, think you can create our opening?" He nodded and took his position at the cannon. "All right, come on, Alex, let's do this." He followed me downstairs. "Stay safe, you guys. See you after I take care of Beelzebub." Alex and I stood by the door and waited. All of a sudden, there was a loud boom, and the door slid open.

"Go, guys. Now's your chance!" Harmony shouted. Alex and I nodded and ran out the door.

"All right, Alex, you and me forever. Let's get these guys!" I shouted. Alex flew above me and pulled off a few circles, engulfing the air around me in flames.

"All right, Sam, you ready to run?" Alex shouted down.

"Let's go, bud!" I shouted back.

"All right then, let's move."

I looked up and kept pace with him as we ran for the castle gate. I heard the demons coming in contact with the flames, but none made it through.

So far so good, but will it hold? I thought.

Have faith in your friend. We will make it to the gate, Tiamat said. *Then we finish Beelzebub off this time, and hopefully that will solve things here.*

You don't think it will?

I didn't say that. I just know that, as of now, he is the main enemy. We just don't know if there are more coming.

"I have us in front of the gate!" Alex shouted, snapping me out of my conversation with Tiamat. "Prepare to fire the professor's weapon on my mark."

I aimed the launcher in front of me.

"Lowering the fire wall in 3...2...1... Now!" he shouted as I watched as the flames vanish. I fired right at the gate.

A ball of swirling colors went flying through the demons in front of us. It landed against the wall at the back of the room in front of us. When it hit the wall, it expanded and began swirling along the wall. The wind picked up, and I watched all the horde demons near it get pulled into the energy and get destroyed. The entrance in front of us was now wide open, as the swirling energy bomb kept pulling any demon that tried to pass into it.

"You ready for this, man?" Alex asked after he landed next to me.

"Yup, let's do this," I said, holding up my arm. He smacked it with his arm, and we nodded before sprinting side-by-side into the castle.

Chapter Twelve

We ran through the halls of the castle trying to locate the throne room. I had my sword out, slicing through the horde demon that we came across. Alex would snipe any that came up behind us with his flames. "That's got to be the path to the throne room ahead!" I shouted as we approached a set of double doors.

"That looks like a good bet to me." Alex nodded as he sniped another demon that came around the corner. We threw ourselves against the giant doors, and they flung open easily. Alex turned around and shut them. He slid the wooden latch between them, preventing the demons from following us in.

"I was wondering if you would make it this far." We both spun around and gazed at a female figure in the shadows of the room. She made its way slowly toward us, and I felt my heart sink instantly.

"Megan?" Alex questioned once she was completely in the light.

"I see you spoiled my plan and saved Alex too," she said to me, ignoring him completely. "You've always been nothing but trouble to me. I knew I couldn't possibly win against you, so when I was approached by Beelzebub and he made an offer, I jumped at the chance." Megan was no longer human. Her body was pitch black from the neck down. The only part that looked human anymore was only her face. "Even though I had turned into this hideous monster, I would still have Alex all to myself. I would finally beat you." She cackled. "Then, once again, you had to ruin it." She began to move her fingers, revealing the claws where her nails used to be. I saw Alex fall to his knees in depression. "Let me tell you, you were close, and Beelzebub is right through that door." She pointed behind her.

"Why are you telling me this?" I asked.

"Because it doesn't matter," she said as wings appeared out of her back. "I will kill you. I will use the strength of this monster you made be become, and I will kill you." She laughed. "Then I will be together with Alex forever!" She jumped at me, and I rolled out of the way, blocking her claws with my sword. I jumped back and tried to get away, but she was on top of me in seconds. I kept blocking her attacks with my sword.

Attack her! Tiamat yelled.

I...can't, I said, still blocking her blows.

Her power is still new to her. She is weak. You know it, he pleaded.

I can't do that to Alex. I glanced to see him still spaced out. *I know that, on some level, he still cares for her. If I kill her, then...*

If you don't kill her, then all this was for nothing! She's not going to let you go, and one of you will have to die. He reasoned.

I know. I answered.

I knew I would have to attack, whether I wanted to or not. I knew Tiamat was right. I jumped back and prepared to strike. That's when flames shot between us. We both turned and looked where they came from. Alex was on his feet, his hands pointed in our direction.

"Sam, go on ahead," he ordered.

"What are you doing, Alex darling?" Megan asked, stunned completely.

"You don't have to do this, Alex." I said.

"Yes, I do!" he said, still aiming at us. "Go, Sam, I promise I will take care of things here."

"But, Alex...," I began to plead. I didn't want him to do this to himself.

"Go, Sam!" he commanded with an anger I hadn't heard ever before. I nodded and took off, bursting through to the throne room.

I entered the throne room, and the door slammed shut behind me. I spun around and tried to open it, but it wouldn't budge. "It's no use, dragon." I spun around at the voice and saw Beelzebub sitting on the throne. "The door is sealed by my magic. No one can open it from either side." He stood up. "It's just you and me now. Your pesky friend, even if he defeats my new pet, cannot interfere."

"I wouldn't ask him to." I stepped away from the door and stepped toward him. "This is a battle destined to be between you and me." I assumed a stance with my sword in front of me.

"There is no destiny for us to fight, dragon," he hissed. "You shouldn't even exist. I should have already opened a portal for my lord and master. I do not know how humans gained the capability to create you, but you have been a pain in my neck. You are just a nuisance to me." He grabbed a lance from a statue by the throne. "It may not be destiny, but I *will* enjoy killing you."

He raised the lance and pointed it at me before bolting straight at me. He struck down with the lance, but I jumped back to slice it off. My blade went right through the lance.

"That blade is powerful. Try this then," the demon said, raising his hand and three mini flies flew at me from behind him. I sliced one in half and deflected a second. The third bit my shoulder. I sliced it in half, but my shoulder began to throb in pain. I quickly slaughtered the third. "That poison will ensure that you die very shortly."

"Haven't you learned by now?" I began while launching an attack. "I am not going to die that easy." I teleported around him, looking for an opening. I found one and spun around at him. He didn't have time to react as I stabbed him in the chest.

"How is this possible?" he cried, stumbling backward, the sword sticking out of him. "I won't…be…killed…by…a…human." He fell backward, lifeless in front of the throne. I grabbed the sword from his chest and began walking back, but then collapsed to my knees; the poison was kicking in.

Well, at least I stopped him, I mentioned, feeling my consciousness beginning to fade. *It's over.*

I don't think it is, Tiamat replied. *You need to stay alive, at least a little longer. I don't think this fight is over yet.*

As if on cue, the entire room began to pulsate like a heartbeat. I forced myself to turn around and saw the floor under Beelzebub swirling. I watched as shadows came from every direction and flew into him, and slowly, he began to erect himself. "Foolish, dragon," he laughed a wicked laugh. "Even though you managed to defeat my demonic body, I will still kill you with the last of my remaining powers." He turned pure black, except for his glowing red eyes. He held out his hand, and I went flying into the wall.

Tiamat shivered within me. *This power. I've never felt anything like it.*

"Is this all you got left?" He walked over and lifted me up with one hand, pinning me against the wall. He hurled me across to the far wall. "Pathetic!" he snarled before walking toward me again.

I struggled to my feet. "I...won't...lose."

"So, you do have fight in you still." He grinned. "I'm glad. No one has forced me to the brink of death before. I'd hate to have it end so soon."

"I will defeat you, Beelzebub. Even at the cost of my life." I said, closing my eyes. *Tiamat, I'm sorry. It's the only way.* I thought of Alex, Harmony, and the others fighting. Then, I focused on the shadow crystal. *Please grant me the power again. I need the strength one final time.* I felt a surge of power flowing through me again. The poison was gone, and I reached full power. I reached my hand out, and my sword returned to me. I saw a look of shock in the glowing eyes of my foe.

"Let's do this then, dragon!" he seethed, flying at me.

"For once, I agree with you." I flew toward him. We met in the air and clashed with incredible force. The windows blew out, and the door flew open. I saw Alex standing there in awe as we fought. Megan's lifeless body was behind him. I felt a quick pang of guilt; I shook it off and focused on the fight. I got a clean shot with my sword and sliced one of his arms off. He hissed and sent me crashing to the wall.

"You will pay for that!" he shouted, flying down and picking up his arm before molding it into a sword. He charged at me, and I deflected the attack with my own.

"I have to admit, that's a nice trick." I went in for an attack, and he deflected mine. "You really are worthy of your position in the demon hierarchy."

"If you think flattery will make me go easy on you, guess again." He jumped back and sent more flies at me. I countered them with my shurikens, destroying them in one full swoop. I launched another wave of shurikens at him, and he jumped up. The shurikens shattered on the throne, causing a crater to be left in its place.

Remember, Sam, this is using your life, Tiamat reminded me. *I don't know how much longer you can keep this up.*

Then let's finish this up then, shall we? I said, deflecting another round of flies with my shurikens. I prayed to the shadow crystal to give me more power. I directed that power into the sword and felt it begin throbbing in my hand. I teleported up above Beelzebub and came down for an overhead strike. Beelzebub brought his sword up to guard. When our swords clashed, mine began to glow, slicing through his blade, shattering it. I jumped off him and came down again, leaving him in shock, and sliced in half.

"Sam, you did it!" Alex ran up, and the castle began to shake and collapse. I grabbed him and teleported outside. The surviving demons began to disappear. "Look, man." He pointed at one of the vanishing demons. "Without Beelzebub, they can't survive here. It really is over."

"I'm sorry," I said as I felt my body beginning to die. I collapsed to the ground in pain.

"Sam?" Alex screamed, picking me up. "Sam, what's happening?"

I tried to answer, but I wasn't even able to talk anymore. My body spasmed in pain.

Loki appeared behind him. "In order to defeat Beezlebub, he willingly gave his life to the shadow crystal," he said.

Hold on, Sam! Tiamat shouted into my mind. *I am going to travel into the crystal and try to separate you again.* I felt Tiamat's presence leave as I transformed back to human. I rolled onto my side and began coughing up blood.

"Sam, you can't die here!" Alex pleaded, holding on to me as I kept coughing up blood. "You actually did it. You prevented the apocalypse. We need to enjoy this…together."

"Your friend will not die." Loki stepped forward and held out his hand. I felt a sharp pain in my chest. I watched as the shadow crystal flew out of my body and into his hand. "I believe this is what Tiamat was trying to do," he smirked.

Tiamat? I called out in my mind. *Come on man, answer me.*

"It's no use trying to talk to Tiamat." Loki grinned. "He went into the crystal to try and save you, and now, I hold the crystal. Your bond is no more."

"Return Tiamat!" I demanded, trying hard to stand up, but failing.

"Sam!" Alex cried out, catching hold of me.

"You should be happy, vessel," Loki smirked. "If I hadn't separated the two of you, you would be dead by now." He held onto the crystal and flashed it at me.

"I promised I would help him." I tried to stand again but couldn't.

"Help him? Help him how? Return home?" He laughed. "Well, in a sense, you will keep your promise." He waved his hand, and a portal appeared in front of him. "He will return to the dragon world, but he will be my slave. Thanks to you, he is in the crystal where I can harness the mighty power of the shadow dragon king. I will use his power to become the ruler of the dragon world." He laughed.

"You lied to us!" Alex yelled.

"No, I didn't!" he bellowed. "I promised to help you prevent the apocalypse, and I did. Thanks to me, you gained the power necessary to defeat Beelzebub. It is time to collect my dues." He stepped into the portal. "Farewell, humans, the time has come for me to write my own destiny. I will rule over my own world." As soon as he stepped through the portal, it vanished into thin air.

"Tiamat!" I cried out before I finally lost consciousness.

Epilogue

"No!" I cried out, letting my tears flow.

"Sam, you're awake." I heard Alex's voice. I opened my eyes and realized I was reclined on a bed. I sat up and saw Alex right beside me.

"How long was I out?" I asked.

"Three weeks," he replied. "I was beginning to really worry."

"Where am I?" I asked looking around in confusion.

"What, you don't recognize your old bed?" He responded in a joking tone, but with concern in his eyes.

"We're home? What happened?" I asked. "The last thing I remember...Loki!" *Tiamat, are you there? Come on, man, answer me!* I began shouting in my head. "He really took him, didn't he?"

"Yeah." Alex nodded, grabbing my hand. "Loki took the shadow crystal from you and Tiamat with it."

"How is everyone else?" I asked, trying to take my mind off Tiamat for the moment.

"They are fine. General Cooshing and Mathers are helping rebuild the city. The professor and Harmony are trying to sort out the wrecked lab and see what can be salvaged."

"The lab was wrecked?"

"Yeah. While we were out, Loki destroyed the lab and took all the research off the computers and destroyed the hard drives. It's like the lab never existed."

"Dammit!" I slammed my fists into the bed. "He played us. I knew he was after something. I just didn't know what. If I only caught on sooner, I could have done something."

"No, you couldn't," Alex said as he held my hand again. "None of us could have done anything. We needed him just as much as he needed us. If it weren't for his help, the casualties would have been much greater. Who knows if we could have stopped them without the soul technology he had given us. He waited until the perfect opportunity to reveal his true colors."

"What now?" I sighed.

"Well, that's up to you," he said. "If you want, General Cooshing said he could pull strings and get us our diplomas, so we are done with high school and can just live in peace. Or…"

"If it's up to me, I want to find a way to get to Tiamat," I blurted out.

"Are you sure?" Alex asked. "If we just leave this be, we can have a peaceful life."

"Alex, he was a part of me," I explained. "I know I didn't have a choice about having him put inside me. I know that he tried to take over. And I know that I *should* let it all go, but I can't. Not only was he my partner, he became a friend. I had never considered him just a tool I could use and throw away. Now, he needs my help. He's in pain with whatever Loki is doing to him."

"He's in pain? How do you know?" Alex asked.

"I can't explain it, man," I shrugged. "I don't know if it's because he was inside of me my entire life. I don't know if it's because we had formed a bond. I don't know if it's because I used the shadow crystal. I just don't know. All I know is that he is in pain." I reached out and pulled Alex in for a hug and let my tears flow free. "He's in pain, and it's because of me. If I hadn't used the crystal like I had, he would never have had to go inside to try and separate me and the crystal."

Alex hugged me back. "You did what you had to do to save us, and he knew that. Besides, I knew you were going to want to do this."

I broke the hug and looked at him. "What do you mean?"

"I knew you would want to go to the dragon world and rescue him," he smiled. "So while you were sleeping, I told Harmony to start looking for a way to reach the dragon world."

"You didn't!" I smiled back.

"Yup, and she says she might have found a way," Alex informed, his chest puffed out with pride. "I'll text her and let her know we will be at the lab, or what's left of it, tomorrow to see what she has found out. You need to get some more rest." He stood up and stretched. "And now that I know you are okay, so do I. I'm going to go sleep in my own bed for a night. See you tomorrow." He started to walk out the door.

"Good night, Alex!" I shouted out.

"Good night, Sam!" he shouted back as I curled back up in my blanket.

The next day, I found myself back in the lab with Harmony and Alex. It was in shambles, pretty much like the rest of the city, but Harmony swore everything was back in working condition. "He may have thought he had ruined all of our research, but I hid the important data on me at all times," she said, pulling her necklace apart to reveal a flash drive inside.

"You think that what's on that will help me get to the dragon world?" I asked.

"That's the plan," she said, plugging the drive into the computer.

"How does research on souls help with dimensional travel?" Alex asked.

"It's not the research on souls that will do it," she said, pulling up a program. "Unknown to Dad even, I decided to start studying Loki."

"You did what?" the professor asked, stepping inside the room.

"Oh chill, Dad," she said, rolling her eyes. "I placed sensors that I had designed within the lab and studied the environment readings from whenever he teleported over." She came over and pricked my finger to get a blood sample and fed it into the computer. "I think I figured out the basics of how Loki gets around, and now if I'm right, a portal should open up behind you...now" She hit a key on the keyboard and a portal appeared at the corner of the room.

"So if I take the portal then…" I began to walk to it.

"You are not taking anything yet!" she shouted, stopping me. "It's not programmed with a location. You take it now, and who knows where you will end up."

"Fair enough," I said, turning around.

"So how are you going to program it?" Alex asked.

"With his blood," she replied, pulling up the program that was reading my blood. There was another reading next to it.

"Whose reading is that?" I asked.

"Yours with Tiamat," she explained. "I'm hoping that I can separate Tiamat's DNA out of your blood and use it to program a location into the portal."

"How?" I asked.

"You wouldn't get it," she dismissed me.

"Burn!" Alex laughed.

"You wouldn't either," she scowled at Alex.

"Ha ha. Who got burned now?" I laughed as he flipped me off. The laughter stopped when the portal changed colors.

"I think I got it," Harmony said, turning toward us.

"So will it take us to the dragon world?" I asked.

"In theory." She nodded.

"Theory?" Alex asked, raising his brow. "That doesn't sound safe at all."

"Hey, there's no real way to test this first," she said. "As far as I can tell, my calculations are sound though."

"That works for me," I said, picking up the supply bag I had packed. I stepped up to the portal and stared into it. I clutched my sword and took a deep breath.

"Hold it!" Alex called, and I stopped.

"Alex, I'm going, and that's that," I said.

"I'm not trying to stop you, but I'm coming with you," he retorted, walking up to stand next to me.

"Look, I appreciate it, but we don't know if this is going to work," I explained. "Even if it does, I have no way of knowing if it's possible to come back. I may be stuck there, and I can't ask you to do that."

"That's exactly why I'm coming with you," he argued. "Look, if this works, you are going to need my help. You don't have a way to fight Loki by yourself."

"I have this," I said, holding up my sword.

"You really think Loki will just let you walk in and kill him with that?" Alex shrugged. "Look, I'm not letting my friend march to his death by himself. I've already lost Megan. I can't lose you too." His eyes welled up, and I finally relented.

"Fine," I sighed and held out my hand. "Together forever, right?"

He took my hand. "Together forever."

"You ready?" I asked, holding his hand and walking to the portal.

"As ready as you are, I think," he replied, laughing.

"All right then." I took a deep breath. "Let's go get Tiamat back." Together with Alex, I stepped into the portal.

About the Author

Nicholas Sumonja was born on March 2, 1988, in Kansas City, Kansas. He has had a passion for writing his entire life, entering every school writing contest that came along. In high school, some of his work was included in a school book of poems and stories. Nick was part of the first graduating class of Olathe Northwest High School in 2006. While there, he continued to develop as a writer along with studying computer animation. He graduated with an endorsement for computer animation on his transcript. Nick currently lives in Blue Springs, Missouri, with his family. He currently works at night and finds time to continue writing stories like this in his free time during the day.